AMIAYA ENTERTAINMENT LLC

Presents

UNWILLING TO SUFFER

A Novel
by
Antoine Inch Thomas

Copyright © 2004 by Antoine Thomas
Written by Antoine Thomas for
Amiaya Entertainment LLC
Published by Amiaya Entertainment LLC
Cover design by Apollo Pixel & Amiaya Entertainment LLC
photograph by Tyrone Grant

Printed in the U.S.A.

ISBN: 0-9745075-2-0

[1. Urban-fiction. 2. Drama-fiction. 3. New York – fiction]

This book was written in F.P.C. Lewisburg 2003

But First
COMING SOON

FROM AMIAYA ENTERTAINMENT LLC

THAT GANGSTA SHIT!

The Anthology

Featuring Stories
by
Antoine Inch Thomas

Here's a Sneak Preview of

CODE OF THE STREETS

Featured in THAT GANGSTA SH!T!

by
Antoine "Inch" Thomas

CHAPTER ONE!

very summer for the past four years, former drug dealer turned community activity planner, Anthony Wheeler, also known as Tone, along with his partner Slick, put together a few events for the urban youth of New York City during Harlem Week. People from all over the place come together and hang out at one designated location. Today the event focused on Renown Charity Organizer, A.I.D.S. Awareness Fundraiser and Community Spokesperson, Flower Moore. Flower was a one-time resident of the Bronx who overcame her own adversities by forming social groups in her current hometown of Reading, Pennsylvania. Flower's priorities focused on domestic issues that were ongoing problems in society. The meetings became such an accomplishment for the twenty-two-year old, she was eventually nominated for two NAACP Awards for Outstanding Achievements of Black Culture two years in a row and was also recognized by Blackpeople Entertainment, Inc. as one of the most prominent figures in urban America. Because of her success, the government, with Flower's permission, adopted her format, created their own program based on her strategies and hired her as president of the organization, providing her with a six-figure salary. In Harlem, specifically 8th Avenue, stretching from 150th to 152nd streets with the blocks cornered off by police barricades, the neighborhood was experiencing an overwhelming sense of well being.

Street vendors were out with their fold out tables blanketed with bootleg merchandise to be sold at a fraction of a price, groups gathered to discuss business and everybody else mingled to their liking.

Tone and Slick had set up the "Flower Moore Rap Off," an event consisting of neighborhood rappers battling one another on a makeshift stage with a cash and prize give-a-way.

Third place winner was to receive $500 cash. Runner up would be taking home $1,000 cash, and the grand prize winner would be given free studio time in Tone's "T&T Entertainment" studio to put together a professional demo tape. Flower, accompanied by her husband Shawn, were among a group of community leaders discussing plans of support groups citywide that concentrated and focused on rape victims and victims of spousal abuse.

A crowd had formed around the stage where some aspiring rappers were about to give their best performances. Standing with his hands clasped behind his back anxiously scanning the rowdy crowd of spectators was *Nappy Black*, a local street rapper who hailed from 140th Street and Lenox Avenue in Harlem. The 5'7", 140 pound, dark complexioned kid dressed in a T-shirt and jeans with short nappy hair had a name that was self-explanatory.

His opponent, a 5'2", 125 pound, fifteen-year-old Puerto Rican kid dressed in oversized navy colored sweatpants, a dingy white T-shirt and a black Doo-Rag wave cap covering his one-week-old corn-rolled braids, called himself *G-Gotti*. G-Gotti's obsession with the late great mob boss, *John Gotti*, was what motivated him to adopt the name. He and Nappy Black went at it as the first two contestants of the Rap Off.

Black grabbed the microphone and confidently began rhyming over an instrumental of a current hip-hop song. The enthusiastic crowd responded by clapping along with the music as the first of the two performers rapped while coasting up and down the stage like he owned it. *"Ayo you claim you G-Gotti/a name that consists of cheese and Fed time and mad dead bodies...You never owned a heater/you never had whips, a crib, a bad bitch, a phone or a beeper..."* The overzealous crowd chanted "oooh's" and "aaah's" as Nappy Black ripped into his opponent lyrically with line after line of disregard and lack of respect for his challenger. *"So how they gon fear it/when San Juan is filled with thugs and big gunz, and you ain't even near it...How you gon prove it/how you gon rep a block with no drugs, and how you gon move it..."* The crowd roared. A friend of Nappy Black climbed on stage almost falling to support his buddy by screaming and shouting how good a performer his friend was and how his adversary, G-Gotti, didn't have a chance.

The beat was reset to its beginning as G-Gotti nervously scanned the crowd and made his way to center stage. Without being given the cue, G-Gotti grabbed the microphone and started his rhyme. *"You claiming you a gangsta, always caught with a chick/and you always making a scene, that's cause you a snitch..."* G-Gotti's first couple of lines sent mixed signals to the crowd. His words were sharp and witty but his delivery wasn't articulate, and realizing his mistake, he became agitated but continued anyway. *"Bitch, you always talking 'bout taking it far/you fake as the hood Jake and you stay getting robbed..."*

With the uneasiness filling the air, G-Gotti lost his self-esteem and ran off the stage.

"Ayo, you heard that bullshit son just kicked?" yelled one male onlooker.

"Word, son was some shit," screamed another youth who was dressed in jeans and a matching denim vest.

"I kind of liked him," I said with my 6'6", 200 pound, tan complexioned self. "I just think he got scared," I continued.

"Yeah, *whatever*. I still think homeboy was wack," said the one spectator who previously stated that the latter of the two performers didn't hold up well.

"Who's up next?" shouted Tone through a bullhorn. "I need my next two challengers up here *now*! We're ready to see somebody else get embarrassed up here on this stage." He continued causing laughter to explode from the exuberant crowd. "Okay, okay! Here we go!" shouted Tone, waving on the next two opponents who just climbed the stage.

Turning to my girlfriend I asked, "Who do you think is going to win this one, Charlene?"

"I'm going for the tall one, Larry," she responded, shortening my name because she said *Lawrence* sounded like a name that belonged to somebody's uncle.

"You're just saying that because you don't like short niggas," I continued.

"Whoever said I didn't like short guys?" Charlene asked, standing in her double-jointed, bowlegged stance, which is what attracted me to the 5'5", 125 pound chocolate beauty contestant in the first place.

"'Cause, I ain't never seen you around any short dudes," I uttered.

"That's because I'm always around *you*, sexy Larry. And you know I love me some Larry. Larry Luuv!" she shouted, screaming and old rap song from the 80s to compliment my name. "La La La, La La La, La La La La, Laarry Luv!" "It's all good. I'm happy. And as soon as I make it to the pro's, everyone else will love me too," I said smiling.

Charlene and I had been dating for the past two years. We loved to hang out, so today we chose to focus our attention on the rappers that had been chosen to rhyme up on the stage. Up next was an aspiring local rapper who called himself *"The Grim Reaper."* The short, heavyset teenager earned his name by lyrically killing all of the opponents he'd rapped against during his lunch periods at school. He, too, began rhyming over a hip hop instrumental.

"Ayo niggas wanna see if I'm right/that's why they ask they lil mans to come hear me, and see if I'm tight...In a minute I'm a be in the sight/of big Benzes and A&R's paying me a fee when I write...So if you niggaz think you real like me/let's go 16 for 16 and see if you appeal like me...if '98 was your meal like me/if you could zone out for Tone, and end up with a deal like me..." The Grim Reaper sang with a confidence level so high that it bordered arrogance. "Yeah, nigga!...What!" he shouted as he jogged around the stage.

"Hold up, hold up!" shouted Tone through his bullhorn. "Aye," he continued. "I like how you slid my name up in your rhyme during your last couple of bars. That was slick, but being *slick* ain't gonna get you anywhere. No pun intended," said Tone looking over at his friend Slick and laughing. "Shorty," shouted Tone looking at the next rapper up for battle, "you gon have to come better than your man right here," said Tone passing *"All*

That" the microphone and signaling to the DJ to start the music. "All That," an average heighted teen with a muscular physique and a tattoo on both of his biceps, walked toward the front of the stage then circled back in his brand new white cotton tank top T-shirt, black jeans and white Air Force One sneakers. "All That" gripped the microphone with the smoothness of a winner.

After Rayshawn's mother purchased him a quarter carat diamond stud earring, he told everyone to call him "All That" because he said Rayshawn wasn't a rap name. Also, all the young ladies that he'd recently been courting due to his newly acquired jewelry, led him to believe that the name suited his personality perfectly. The kids in his neighborhood, on the other hand, respected his moniker because his rap style appeared to be more advanced and unique than the other young street rappers in his neighborhood.

As "All That" took to the stage, his eyes told the crowd that he commanded his position, and the words that came out of his mouth confirmed this truth.

"Ayo check how I'm strong on the bricks, dog of the click/my second win and never got along with a snitch...I'm often the kid, in the cut chump, offing that clip/take it to your wake and toss it in that coffin you in...You assed out like a thong on a chick, mourn if you would/it's bodies in the Jects like a morgue in the hood...Boss of the streets, kid wit my name in the biz/my neck so cold, I gotta keep my chain in the fridge...Flop never, a Champion, I stay wit a gig/And Rock Fellas like I'm Jay-Z or Damon and Biggs, Holla..."

The crowd went into a frenzy as *"All That"* gave the spectators punch line after punch line of true raw talent.

"Fifty! That's the next fucking 50 Cent!" screamed ~~Tone~~ as he made his way from the side of the stage back to where the microphone stand was set up. "Holla at me son! Word up. Holla at me, you heard!" continued Tone as everyone dispersed into their own private little groups commenting on the talented young aspiring rap artists.

"Charlene, walk me to the Chinese restaurant. I'm fiending for some Chicken and Broccoli," I said, walking toward 153rd Street and 8th Avenue where a nearby Asian restaurant had a section of it carved out for customers who like to sit down and eat.

Charlene twisted up her lip and gave me a stink look to indicate that she noticed how self-assured I was about myself. She fixed her face and asked me to slow down as she trotted to catch up to me. She grabbed my hand, looked at the side of my face and asked, "Do you love me, Larry?" Her teeth had grown in evenly making her smile something to look at. Charlene was always persistent with her line of questioning, and she showed it as we waited for our orders. "Larry!" she quietly shouted. "Do you love me?"

Familiar with her persistence, I answered, "Yes, damn! What's gotten into you? You act like you don't know how I feel or something. Come on, Ma, you know I love your ass to death," I said grabbing, hugging and kissing her on her lips and forehead.

Outside, a black conversion van with tinted windows pulled up right in front of *"Mr. Lee's Chinese Takeout."* In front and behind the van were four Ford Explorer's with tinted windows. All five vehicles were outside of the 153rd Street eatery as Charlene and I stood inside enjoying our conversation. We waited on our food, totally oblivious to the convoy that sat right outside. All 16 doors of the vehicles swung open as several plain clothes officers ran inside the restaurant and aimed their heavy artillery at my face and at Charlene.

"Get down! Get on the fucking floor now!" screamed the lieutenant in charge.

Everyone in the store including Charlene and myself immediately dropped to the floor and placed our hands on the back of our heads.

"Is this him?" asked the lieutenant talking into his two-way radio as he kept his A.T. 9MM rifle pointed at my head. I knew the make and model of the gun because a friend of mine had one just like it.

"Stand him up and face him toward our direction," said the voice over the walkie talkie.

"Get up!" said the lieutenant, keeping his gun pointed at me. Charlene was on the ground beside me crying and shaking.

When I stood up, the lieutenant grabbed me and brought my hands down behind my back. He led me near the large restaurant window that provided potential customers with an eyeful of what was on Mr. Lee's gourmet menu and told me to face outside. Holding me firmly as I faced the street, the lieutenant spoke into his radio. "Is this the suspect, sir, yes or no?"

"Hold on," said the voice over the radio.

The silence that filled the air made it seem like one could hear a mouse piss on cotton. The few seconds it took for confirmation felt like a lifetime.

"10-4," said the voice, then the walkie talkie went dead.

"Cuff him! Cuff his ass!" yelled the lieutenant to his assisting officers.

"Yo, what the fuck are y'all taking me for?" I screamed as I struggled with the small army of officers.

"Get off of him!" muffled Charlene who, as she tried her best to help me, was quickly subdued by two female officers. "Leave it alone, young lady! Leave it alone! ... Now!" screamed one of the female officers who had Charlene in a chokehold.

"Just call my moms. Call my ...," I yelled as I was dragged and thrown into the backseat of a waiting patrol car.

The officers kept their guns drawn as they slowly exited the oriental takeout. As quickly as they came, we were gone.

Charlene struggled to open up her purse and retrieve her cellular phone as the tears from her eyes temporarily blurred her vision. Dialing my home number, the telephone was answered on the third ring.

Ring...Ring...Ring!

"Hello, Mrs. Robinson speaking," answered my mom sounding very proper ever since talent scouts had begun calling our home showing an interest in my performance on the court.

"Ma, Larry got locked up!" shouted Charlene into the phone over her tears.

"Noooo!" screamed Mrs. Robinson.

CHAPTER TWO!

In another section of the city, the sun illuminated the sky as Curtis Martin and his mother, Danielle, prepared to leave their home.

"Curtis," said Mrs. Martin, calling her son in a cordial, relaxed manner. She looked in her purse to reassure herself that she had everything she needed. She made sure her keys, her money and the coupons she spent all week cutting from the newspapers were tucked into her small pocketbook. Closing her handbag, she looked toward the staircase that led to the second floor of her Queens home and called out to her son once again. "Curtis."

"Yes, Mom," replied Curtis in a respectful manner.

"Are you ready to take me shopping?" she kindly asked, looking up the steps.

"One second, Mom. I'll be right down," he said, keeping his tone leveled at a respectable note.

Curtis was a twenty-three-year-old drug dealer who lived with his mother in their Queens home. At 5'9", he had an average build weighing about 175 pounds. His chestnut complexion is what attracted most women to him, and his flawless skin is what locked them in. He had almond shaped eyes with thick eyebrows and a thin mustache.

Mrs. Martin was still young and looked even younger. She was sixteen when she birthed Curtis. After his father left for the war, she never bore another child because her husband never returned. Derrick Martin was considered missing in action two months after his arrival in the country of Afghanistan. When a year had passed and still no word from the Middle East, Derrick was considered a Casualty of War. His wife was presented with his medal of honor. A sergeant from the United States Marines knocked on Mrs. Martin's door one morning when Curtis was just four months old and awarded her his Purple Heart for Bravery. She framed it and let it hang in her living room next to her father's photo. He, too, died fighting a war that to everyone else who wasn't a soldier of the United States seemed senseless, worthless and very expensive.

After stuffing ten thousand dollars in each one of his front pants pockets, Curtis put on one of his oversized button up Polo shirts. The three sizes too big allowed him the ability to easily conceal the bulges that jutted out from his trousers. Looking in his full-length mirror, Curtis turned his body from side to side making sure his attire looked normal and presentable. The half smile and popping of his collar was physical affirmation that he was set to go.

Carefully trotting down the stairs, Curtis hit the automatic start on his brand new Ford Expedition, then affectionately yelled to his mother, "I'm ready, Mom."

Closing her bible, Mrs. Martin placed the Good Book back on their dining room table, slid herself to the edge of the sofa and stood up while simultaneously saying, "About time." She grabbed her purse and walked toward their front door where Curtis kindly held both the wooden and screen doors for her.

She walked past him, nodded her head and said, "Thank you, sweety." She eased her way down the porch steps using the handrail as a reinforcement.

Curtis locked both the sturdy wooden and frail screen doors of their home and quickly ran to the passenger side of the SUV to assist his mother entering the large vehicle.

"I'm okay, Curtis baby. Just bring your butt on in so we can get going," she said in the sweetest voice. Mrs. Martin practically lived for Jesus Christ, so everything she did or said, she tried to do it in the name of her Lord and be as warm and sincere as possible about it.

Curtis turned on the passenger side overhead television and pulled down the visor exposing a 6"x6" color television monitor. Looking over at his mom, he asked, "Do you want to watch *Big Momma's House?*" Curtis was referring to an urban comedy starring acclaimed comedian *Martin Lawrence.*

Looking like she could pass for his sister or girlfriend, Mrs. Martin replied by saying, "I'm okay. I'll enjoy the scenery as we coast down the boulevard."

"Okay," he replied. He flipped the visor back up and the two of them peacefully rolled down Queens Boulevard listening to the sweet sounds of *Luther Vandross.*

After driving for a few minutes, Curtis noticed the signal he'd been looking for. Two blocks up on the right, a man held up a homemade sign that read, "Car Wash $10.00."

"Mom," said Curtis softly, "I'm going to pull over here for one second."

"Boy, I know you're not going to wash this truck again. You just washed it yesterday," said Mrs. Martin observing the guy holding the sign. Normally, she would've overlooked the stunt as just another black man trying to get his hustle on legitimately, but the diamonds that glistened on the guy's wristwear caused her to analyze the scene more carefully.

"I'm not washing this truck again. I forgot to grab some air fresheners," said Curtis looking over at his mom. Once they caught eye contact, he turned his attention to his rear view mirror on which he then placed his hand indicating that it was lacking its usual fragrance ornament.

His mother looked at him and a feeling of relief took over her body causing her to smile and say, "Just hurry up back. Mommy wants to get to Pathmark before it gets crowded."

With that, Curtis exited the jeep and walked over to his waiting associate.

"What up, son," said the young black guy holding out his hand requesting their usual ghetto handshake as a friendly gesture.

"If he's the guy, shake his hand, then give him a hug. And I thought you said he operates alone. It seems he brought along his girlfriend," said an undercover Alcohol, Tobacco and Firearms agent looking through the lenses of his high-powered binoculars. Hearing the agent speak through a mini microphone which transmitted his voice to a small earbud in his ear, Curtis' associate was able to act out everything that he was told. The agents had set up a sting operation to get Curtis on a buy and bust sale, but since Curtis was now accompanied by someone, what was supposed to be a simple sale, had now become a conspiracy.

Looking around observing everything normal and suspicious, Curtis' preoccupation blurred his view and he didn't notice the cable company van parked directly across the street.

His sixth sense was preprogrammed by the law enforcement television shows he saw everyday on T.V., so all he was prepared for was zeroing in on dark colored Crown Victorias or Chevrolet Caprices. "What are you all happy about, son. You're all touchy feely and shit today for some reason." Curtis sensed something wasn't right, but the irresistible smile his contact had sprawled across his face made him dismiss any foul play.

"Give me a hug, my nigga!" said his associate.

Curtis hugged the guy establishing himself as the target.

"You got the dough?" asked the guy, referring to the buy money as they separated from their embracement.

"Yeah, when do you want it? Not here in the open," said Curtis looking around.

Sighing, the guy said, "Nah, dog. Of course not out here. Just act like you're looking inside this van right here," said the contact pointing to a multicolored conversion van. "The coke is sitting on the front seat. Just exchange it with the money and I'll holla at you later. Cool?" asked the connect nervously. Before he allowed Curtis to answer, he added, "Oh yeah, you gave me $200 extra last time and since your money is always rubber banned up, instead of removing it from what you just brought me, I left the two bills sitting next to the work."

"Yeah, yeah. Okay," said Curtis walking over to the van.

The van was equipped with a camera that was placed into the face of the radio. As most men would do when entering a vehicle, Curtis entered the van through the passenger side which wasn't facing any traffic, looked at the package of cocaine, then looked at the stereo in the van where his face was being recorded.

"As he's driving off, throw your right hand in the air and

wave goodbye to your friend. That will be our signal to move and you better not pull no fast one on us or our deal won't be worth diddly," said the agent.

Curtis exited the van, gave the guy another handshake and headed to his vehicle. He hopped back in his truck, wrapped the air fresheners around the rear view mirror and said, "Mom, do you need this?" he asked holding up two one-hundred dollar bills.

"Curtis, where'd you get that?" asked Mrs. Martin with a concerned look on her face. She looked at her son and squinted her eyes in tight slits and said, "I told you about getting money from those guys."

"Mom, I told you they still owed me from a long time ago. I'm not in the streets anymore. I told you, I'm finished." Curtis didn't know the latter part of his sentence was true—*he was finished.*

Mrs. Martin grabbed the money from her son's hand, but his words had fallen on deaf ears. Mrs. Martin was fed up with her son's lying. She was unaware of the transaction, but in a few moments, everything would all come to light.

Pulling off, Curtis heard his friend yell, "Ahight, yo!"

Curtis put his hand out the window forming a peace sign with his pointer and middle fingers causing his associate to react by raising his own hand giving the officers their cue to handle their business.

Mel Drake's side of the deal was done. Mel had been arrested the night before for driving while intoxicated. The DWI summons led to an impound of his vehicle. When his Mercedes Benz entered the police impound lot, the skillfully trained canines immediately descended upon the trunk of his $80,000 car signifying that drugs were present. A subsequent search ended with the police retrieving two 9mm semiautomatic handguns, 200 rounds of ammunition and a half pound of marijuana. Mel was so afraid of going to prison that he spilled the beans on his marijuana connections and his cocaine dealings. The authorities asked him what would he be willing to do or give them in exchange for his freedom. Without hesitation, he said *Curtis Martin*.

As Curtis drove off, a multitude of squad cars descended upon his automobile with guns raised in the air.

"Don't fucking move, Curtis Martin!" yelled an officer approaching the car with his gun raised. "And tell your lady friend to do the same. Tell her to stop moving, now!" he screamed.

Mrs. Martin was nervous, so she began shaking uncontrollably. She had never seen a gun in real life, only on television.

"Grab her and retrieve whatever it was that Curtis handed to her," said the officer motioning with his weapon to a female officer standing nearby.

The female cop walked over to the side of the vehicle, opened the door and dragged Mrs. Martin to the ground. As she pleaded for help, three more officers went to the aid of their coworker and helped restrain the woman. Pulling the two one-hundred dollar bills from Mrs. Martin's purse, the female officer yelled, "I got it!"

"Is it marked?" said a voice over her radio.

Flipping it over, the lady cop recognized two red lines that were strategically placed at the left hand corners of the bills. She pressed the side button of her radio, brought it to her face and gleefully said, "It's marked."

"10-4," the other voice responded. She placed her walkie talkie back on her belt, lifted Mrs. Martin from the ground, aggressively brought her hands down behind her back, cuffed her and said, "Take her too."

The officers led Curtis to an awaiting squad car and violently shoved him into the back seat.

By this time, Mrs. Martin had gotten a hold of herself and stopped hollering. She figured this was all a mistake and possibly racial profiling, and as soon as they reached the precinct, everything would be figured out.

Curtis peered out the back window of the police cruiser and caught eye contact with his mother who was in another cruiser twenty feet away. With tears forming in the corners of his eyes, Curtis moved his lips mouthing the words, *"I love you, Mom. I'm sorry."*

Mrs. Danielle Martin, who never saw her son in such a desperate state of anguish, took on a worrisome and fearful look herself. Her eyes were wide and the tears never stopped falling. When one of the officers hit the sound button on his squad car, the lights flashed and the siren began screaming, bringing the reality of what just transpired to an even more elevated level. Mrs. Martin jumped in her seat and focused her eyes on the officers who now entered the vehicle that she occupied. The assisting officer turned around, looked at Mrs. Martin like if he cared and said, "What a shame." He turned back around, took off his hat, placed it on the dashboard and pulled the built in computer closer to him. As he began typing digits into the small keyboard, Mrs. Martin glanced back over to her son who was now being driven away. The car she was in jerked as the senior officer brought the vehicle out of *"Park"* and placed it in the

"Drive" position.

As if everything were rehearsed, all the patrol cars raced down Queens Boulevard in unison, one behind the other, all headed to police headquarters.

What began as a beautiful, lovely summer afternoon now seemed like an ugly, repulsive nautical day. And it was just the beginning.

CHAPTER THREE

As I sat in an empty room of the 51st precinct located on 147th Street and Edgecomb Avenue, I could hear telephones ringing, typewriters popping non-stop and the occasional sound of static coming from the speakers of police radios. My wrist began to hurt from the position that my arm was in because I was handcuffed to a metal bar that sat two feet higher than the bench that I took refuge in. I guess you could call it a holding cell because it was damp, cold, and it possessed your customary toilet/sink combination.

It didn't have the traditional bars like the jail cells you would see on television. Instead, it had a steel door with a small window located at the center of it. My bladder was full and my stomach ached from emptiness. I should've been thinking about why I was being held, but the only thing that came to my mind, however, was the order of chicken and broccoli that I was waiting on when I got arrested.

After being held in that room for *I don't know how long*, the turning of the lock let me know that the games were about to begin.

As the door opened, I could see a figure being led down a nearby hallway with some type of cloth covering his or her head.

I didn't know whether the individual had anything to do with me or not, but I did watch enough television shows that dealt with law enforcement to understand that the possibility existed that I was allowed to *see* what I *saw* for a reason. A white officer that seemed as cordial as one of the guys at my church undid my handcuffs and led me to another room which was set up like the interrogation rooms I'd seen on shows like *"NYPD Blue"* and *"Law & Order."* I didn't feel guilty of anything because I knew I hadn't done anything, but my natural instincts caused me to recollect on things that I may have done in the past. My palms were sweaty and my knees were weak because I was nervous, but as a child, I used to lie to my parents sometimes to get things that I wanted which enabled me to maintain a look that made me appear calm on the surface.

In came the *"peanut gallery"* dressed in their designer cotton trousers and loosened up ties giving me the notion that we were going to be there for a while. Two detectives sat right across from me whipping out their ballpoint pens and yellow legal notepads while two uniformed officers stood in the corners of the room that I couldn't see, because my back was facing them.

"Good afternoon, Mr. Robinson, I'm Homicide Detective Tom Morano," said the 5'9", 180 pound detective. Folding his hands on the table, the detective continued. "And this is my partner, Richard Burns," he said, introducing his partner who resembled Detective Morano except his partner had a receding hairline.

I kept quiet because I knew my rights and I knew I didn't have to say anything if I didn't want to.

"Mr. Robinson, as you know, you're not under arrest," said

Morano straightening up in his seat. "Just cooperate with us and we'll make everything go as smoothly as possible." He brought his hands together and rested them on the table in front of him.

I remained quiet. I just sat there staring at the detective like if I was trying to read his mind. I guess he got uncomfortable because he kept squirming in his seat until he figured we wasted enough time.

"Mr. Robinson, a little over a month ago, the fourth of July to be exact, could you by any chance recall where you were, from let's say 6 p.m. till around midnight?" asked the detective, tapping his pen and looking me in my eyes. I guess he was looking for signs indicating that I was lying or about to lie, but as I learned in my childhood years, if I stay calm, I'll be ahight.

I raised up from my slouched position and looked the detective in his face noticing a small bruise between his nose and upper lip. I figured he received it shaving his mustache earlier that day, but since it wasn't my concern, I simply said, "None of your business. And I ain't saying shit else unless my attorney is present."

I presumed the detective knew my tough guy attitude was all a bluff because he came running around the table like a mad man and put his hands all up in my face. "Larry, you listen here, young man!" he yelled. "Now I'm not playing around. You're in *my* damn precinct and I'll do whatever the hell I want to without being questioned. You piece of shit! You play this innocent college basketball crap but I ain't buying into it! I've seen your kind before." He continued yelling at me becoming more furious. Standing with only about an inch of distance between us, I never blinked. "You act like you're this good kid. You carry a basketball in one hand and a pistol in your waistband. Now tell me, Larry, where the hell were you on the night of July 4th?"

It was clear that he was pissed off because at this point, he had the majority of my shirt balled up in his hands. I couldn't take the humiliation. Plus, I figured, if I just tell this pig the truth, which is what I thought he wanted to hear, maybe we could get all of this over with as soon as possible. So I complied.

"I was at a motel getting some pussy. There! You happy?" I think my answering him eased him a bit because he let go of my shirt. He drilled me after that.

"With who?" he asked, making his way back around the table and finding his seat.

"You don't know her. She don't fuck with white boys," I said sarcastically.

Then Officer Burns cut in. He'd been quiet the entire time. But as a team, Burns knew it was his time to shine.

"What motel?" asked Detective Burns, leaning toward me as he rested his palms on the table.

"This lil hole in the wall joint on 145th Street," I said referring to a privately owned tenement building that illegally operated as a $20 per hour love haven.

"With who?" asked Detective Morano. They were trying to confuse me going back and forth.

"One of my shorties," I said, not wanting to divulge any names so as to avoid involving anyone else.

"Her name. Give me her name!" screamed Burns.

"Joanne," I said.

"Joanne what?" asked Morano.

"Joanne gives-some-good-ass-head, that's what," I said surprising myself with the joke and sarcasm.

The detectives leaned in toward me indicating that they meant business and weren't there to play any games.

"I don't know her last name," I said as I turned my head. By this time, I was beginning to feel uncomfortable.

"You sleeping with a woman that you don't even know?" asked Morano.

"Nah, I know her, I just don't know her last name. Her last name ain't an issue with me. Her lips are," I said smiling.

"Who signed for the room?" asked Detective Burns.

"You don't have to sign for any rooms at that spot. You just give the dude in charge a 20 spot, get the key, and go and handle your business. Simple as that," I said, looking at Burns who was now sitting on the table.

"So no one signed for the room?" asked Morano.

"No. I just told you *no*, right?" I said becoming frustrated myself.

"So no one can verify your whereabouts for the 4th of July?" asked Burns.

"Yeah," I said, "*I* can!"

"Well, you said this guy charges $20 an hour. What hour time frame did you guys occupy the room?"

"I copped the joint for the whole night," I said, meaning I rented the room for the entire evening. I continued. "Homie gave me a deal because I know him."

"Oh, *now* you know him? What do you do, sell him crack?" asked Detective Burns trying my nerves.

"I don't sell drugs, homie. I play ball and fuck bitches."

I guess I struck a nerve in the detective because Morano leaned back into my face closer than he had the first time and said, "Listen, boy! I'm not your homie or one of your little street thug friends. There was a shooting at a party on 149th Street and Seventh Avenue and we have a witness who placed you at the scene. This witness also said he saw you shoot this kid several times near the side of the building. Now you mean to tell me that you was laid up in some illegal motel with some girl named Joanne that you don't even know, for the entire night, for $20, and you have no way to prove it?" Backing off and rolling up his sleeves, he continued. "I believe your girlfriend is in the lobby of our precinct and according to our records," said the detective flipping through his pocket notepad, "her name is Charlene Portis, not Joanne. Can you explain that, Larry?"

"Yeah, I can explain that," I said, leaning toward the detective. "I wasn't hitting wifey that night. I was sliding up in my lil down low shorty," I said explaining to the detective in street slang that I was cheating on my girlfriend.

"Really?" he asked.

"Yes, *really*," I kindly answered.

"Well, do you know anything about a kid getting shot that night?" he continued picking.

The streets talk so I heard about what allegedly happened that evening. I felt it would be no big deal to say some of what I knew because I really *didn't* know exactly what happened, but I *did* know who pulled the trigger. Everyone in the hood did as well. I knew the incident took place and I had heard details about how and why it went down. So I said, "I heard about it."

"What did you hear, Larry?" asked Morano, rubbing his chin as he paced the room.

I began to believe that every time the detective thought he had something, he would refer to me by name. So now I figured dude thought he had a crack in his already loose case.

"I heard some Spanish kid from the Bronx somewhere was at a party in my neighborhood and was acting up," I said crossing my arms. I had this awkward feeling that sort of felt good knowing that even though I wasn't directly involved in any of the gritty street antics that took place in my neighborhood, there were people who made sure our neighborhood wasn't violated by anyone.

"What do you mean, '*acting up?*'" asked Detective Burns knowing exactly what I meant.

"I heard he was fronting. Telling dudes they couldn't enter the premises because they were black."

"Well what happened after that?" continued Detective Burns.

"I really don't know," I said, trying to illustrate in my head what might've happened. "I guess dudes wasn't trying to hear that bullshit. They said the kid came downstairs still on that racist shit and started walking around with his gun out like he owned our hood."

"So he had a gun on him?" asked Detective Morano looking at my hands.

"Yeah, he had his heat on him," I said with confidence. "But they said he must've forgot that he wasn't wearing a vest because all that fronting got him sent back to the essence."

"So, his behavior wasn't tolerated by your crew so you guys killed him," said Morano staring at me looking for something.

Mrs. Robinson didn't raise no dummy. I was already prepared for his tricky questioning and reversed psychology.

"From what I hear, his behavior *wasn't* tolerated. And *no*, I *don't* have a crew and I *didn't* kill anybody, if that answers your question," I said.

"Who shot him with the 22 caliber, Larry?" he immediately shot his question at me.

I heard the kid from the neighborhood who shot the guy used a forty-five semiautomatic, so now I was sure that these toy cops didn't know what they were talking about. Now it's my time to start busting people's bubble. So I thought.

"He didn't get shot with a 22. He got hit up with a four pound. 4.5 baby. Blew his fucking melon back."

The detective gave me that look of confidence again and my name was the first thing that came out of his mouth. "Larry, no one knew what kind of gun this kid Louis Gonzalez was killed with except our coroner and our forensics office. That's a vital piece of information, Larry," said Morano matter-of-factly.

"Especially if you weren't present at the time of the shooting," said Burns looking at me with his hands in his pockets.

Bursting through the door like a S.W.A.T. team making a raid, a heavyset black guy dressed in a dark suit to camouflage his 240 pound frame entered the room and made his presence immediately known. Peering down on me with his beedy, dark brown eyes, small Afro, thick connecting eyebrows and Richard Pryor mustache, Sergeant Dennis Sherman delivered the terrifying, unfortunate news I had been hoping to avoid all day.

"Morano, Burns," he looked at the detectives. "I just got a call from Judge Burich at 100 Centre Street two minutes ago. Our witness testified before a Grand Jury and the people returned an indictment," said the sergeant, holding a sheet of paper that he pulled from his fax machine just moments ago. He looked over at me and shook his head in disbelief, then turned back to his subordinates and began reading from his paper. My heart dropped before the first word left his mouth and I just knew I was going to vomit at that very moment. The lack of food prevented me from throwing up, but the sergeant's next words almost caused me to move my bowels right there where I sat. "Under indictment #1536-02, Mr. Lawrence Robinson, you will hereby be formally charged with the murder of Louis Gonzalez on July 4, 2002 on the following counts."

I heard the first count, but I must've went into a deep shock because count one was the only count I thought I had until I went in front of the judge for arraignment. When the sergeant read the counts to me, had I been conscious and not on cloud nine, I probably would've heard him say, "*Count one*, 125.25 Murder in the second degree; *Intentional Murder. Count two*, 125.20 Murder in the second degree; *Depraved Indifference. Count three*, 120.20 *Manslaughter in the first degree. Count four*, 120.15, *Manslaughter in the second degree. Count five*, 230.40 *Possession of a weapon in the first degree. Count six*, 230.35 *Possession of a weapon in the second degree* and *Count seven*, 310.80 *Reckless Endangerment in the first degree*."

I realized I was still in the interrogation room when Detective Burns pulled me out of the chair to go and finger-print me. "I can't believe this shit is happening to me," I thought. "*Murder? Not the kid. Not Larbury.*" They had to fingerprint me over and over at least three times because I had no feeling in my hands or feet. I'm surprised I stood up long enough for them to get anything out of me.

I was eventually read my rights and placed in an official holding cell with prison bars. My arraignment was set for 9 o'clock that evening and I was finally given something to eat. Two sandwiches, a milk and an old rotten apple. One of the sandwiches had only cheese in between its slices. The other sandwich had two slices of mystery meat in between its slices. I think I ate everything all at once because my mind went blank after that.

I can imagine how I looked all alone in that cold cell that evening, like a homeless man in his homemade cardboard Condo.

CHAPTER FOUR!

esting in a police precinct in the Kew Garden section of Queens, the couple sat uncomfortably in separate interrogation rooms. Curtis sat perched with his back slightly slumped and his arms crossed. His lips were contorted as if he were expressing his disbelief of what happened, but his eyes told another story. His eyes said to anyone who looked that this young man was scared.

Staring at nothing in particular on the table in front of him, Curtis' eyes never seemed to have blinked. The skin between his eyes was puckered and wrinkled from the agitated look that seemed to sit easily on his face.

Mrs. Danielle Martin, on the other hand, sobbed uncontrollably. The desperate feeling of not knowing is what affected her most. She would look toward the door whenever she heard the noise of someone walking by and her eyes would search the room when the commotion got louder. Paranoia was nothing, Mrs. Martin was terrified. The events that lay ahead would only determine how strong Mrs. Martin and her son really were.

Entering Curtis' room were four men. Their grand entrance snapped Curtis out of his momentary trance and back into reality. He observed each man carefully as if his visual analysis could determine what each man was thinking. It wasn't surprising that one of the four officers was black either. The way Curtis perceived it, they needed someone who could possibly get him to talk. The same strategy they pulled with Mel Drake. However, they way the authorities looked at it, Curtis was going to talk regardless.

The quartet sat on the opposite side of the table and as Curtis suspected, the black man spoke first.

Looking down at the defendant's paperwork, the 6'2", 220 pound, baldheaded detective read over the charges to himself, and in the rear of his mind he thought, *"Another one of my brothers chasing a lost cause."* He placed the papers back on the table and began to speak. Their eyes never connected with one another, but both men could see how the other one felt. "Mr. Martin, do you understand the seriousness and severity of the charges brought against you?" he asked, only glancing at the defendant.

Curtis straightened his arched back, stopped fidgeting with his fingers, peered at the detective and softly replied, "Can I call my lawyer?"

Prepared that the young man would say that, the black officer pulled himself closer to the table, tilted his head slightly sideways and calmly spoke. "You can call an attorney, if you can get to a telephone. But from what I see," said the detective holding his hands out on the table signifying that his palms were empty, while simultaneously looking around the room, "there aren't any phones here." Returning back to his relaxed position, the large black cop continued to talk. "Listen, Curtis, I know you're a smart kid. And smart kids make wise decisions. What you need to decide now is if you're willing to let your mother suffer for your misbehavior." After giving it a thorough check, it was confirmed that Mrs. Danielle Martin was indeed Curtis' mother and not one of his female associates as the cops had assumed. "You involved your mother in this. It wasn't us." Once again leaning closer and lowering his voice, the detective continued. "Make the decision right now, and you and your mom walk. Right now, right this moment, and I can make all of this disappear," said the detective explaining everything with his hands. "It's up to you, Curtis. The ball is in your court. Tell us who buys the coke from you, we investigate your lead, you make the confirmation and we make the arrest."

With a smirk on his face, Curtis quickly shot back. "So basically all I have to do is tell you guys who I deal with. You know, help you guys set him up like Mel set me up," said Curtis smiling now, "testify against him in a court of law if he decides to take it to trial, and my mother and I can walk free?" He raised his brow to indicate that he wanted an answer.

"You guys walk right out that door," said the officer pointing toward the door with confidence.

"Well, here's what I'm willing to give you," said Curtis preying on the man's hunger and feeding his famine ego a bunch of crap. "I'm willing to give your Uncle Tom ass the finger," said Curtis counting on his fingers beginning with his middle, "and another opportunity to allow me to contact my lawyer. Now one thing is for sure and that is, Mrs. Martin's son ain't no fucking rat. So leave me alone with that snitching bullshit." Then Curtis returned to his slouched sitting position.

Fed up at the conclusion that Curtis wasn't going to work with them, the detective slid his chair backward, stood up and walked toward the door. Once he reached the door with his three stooges in tow, he turned back toward Curtis and said, "You're a young kid, Curtis, don't wait until it's too late."

The officers exited the room and left Curtis drowning in the words that were last spoken. He leaned his head back, looked toward the ceiling and thought to himself, *"I'll take the rap for this. A lil ten years ain't shit. There's light at the end of that tunnel. And hopefully, my mom will forgive me one day for this mess."*

A female officer exited the room that Mrs. Martin was being held in as the foursome headed her way. With an exhausted look on her face, Officer Carla Jiminez stood with her back to the door and crossed her arms as the small group of men approached her area. She began to speak as Detective Steve Todd braced himself for the unacceptable news.

"Todd, I don't think she knows anything," said Officer Jiminez shrugging her shoulders.

"Well, what's her story?" asked Detective Todd crossing his huge arms.

"She maintains her story that she was simply on her way grocery shopping. I...I mean, she still has the coupons she cut out and they all matched the items she wrote down on her grocery list." Dropping her arms and sighing, she sympathetically asked, "What do we do with her? I think she's innocent."

The detective looked at Officer Jiminez and said, "It's simple." He brushed past her, opened the door of the room where Mrs. Martin sat crying and walked over to her. Towering over the poor lady, Detective Steve Todd exhaled and thought to himself, *"I hate this job."* He then proceeded to read Mrs. Danielle Martin her rights. "Mrs. Danielle Martin, you are under arrest for conspiracy with intent to sell 1,000 grams of powder cocaine. You have the right to remain silent." He continued as Mrs. Martin buried her head in her hands and began weeping uncontrollably. She jerked every time the words, *"You have the right to,"* slipped from the detective's mouth. "You have the right to an attorney. If you cannot afford one, one will be appointed to you." The words slid out of the detective's mouth with an echoing effect. Detective Todd peered down at Mrs. Martin like if he were about to answer her cries for help, and before he could let her childlike aura take a toll on him, he knelt down near her ear and whispered, "I'll do whatever I can to convince your son to make the right decision. Hopefully, you'll be able to help me out. I'm sorry, Mrs. Martin," said the detective patting her softly on her shoulder. He stood up, turned and left the room.

en I call your name, give me your I.D. number and address." Ms. Jackson, a short broad with a super fat ass and a long weave ponytail was admitting us from court into the *"Receiving and Departure"* area of the *"Beacon"* on Riker's Island. We arrived around 11 o'clock that evening, but due to an incident in one of the housing units, myself and the other two inmates that were also being admitted had to wait patiently on the prison bus in the parking lot until a little after midnight.

Ms. Jackson, with her ghetto pretty self proceeded with the names, "Colon!"

"Ayo!" yelled the other guy that was with us. The Spanish kid, Colon, was knocked out and I guess homeboy that was with us had a little less patience than the Colon cat and I.

Colon jumped up out of his sleep with his hands cuffed in front of him and said, "Yo!" Had I not known any better, I would've thought this Colon guy was a crackhead by the way his eyes protruded from his head. But then again, he just woke up.

"Your I.D. number and address?" You could tell that Ms. Jackson had done this many times before because it was no sweat off her brow that the Spanish kid was wasting time.

"Que?" he said.

"Your fuckin' name, nigga!" said our third passenger. "That's why I hate y'all *German* ass niggaz. Ma'fuckas can sell us all that coke, but you can't speaky no English." Then the guy looked at Ms. Jackson and said, "Tell him you want some *pedico* and I bet you he'll answer your ass in English then." He looked over at Colon.

Ms. Jackson had to be tough to be a C.O. on Riker's Island. But like anybody, when something funny is said, someone's going to laugh. Ms. Jackson chuckled at *Mr._"Antsy's"* remarks but remained patient.

I figured it was time for me to step in because I was starving, tired and I really wanted to lay my ass down. So I interjected, "Como se llamo?" Everybody looked at me like I was crazy. But I turned right to *Mr. "Rude Ass"* and said, "School nigga! I took up Spanish my sophomore and junior years. Ever heard of it?" I asked homeboy with a touch of sarcasm. *Shit, I was on the Island, a nigga had to be hard_to survive on the Rock.*

"Ever heard of what, nigga?" Dude was all in my face, but I knew wasn't anything going down. We were all still handcuffed.

"School, ma'fucka!"

"What!" He was even closer in my face than before. And Ms. Jackson's ass still hadn't intervened.

"Tranquilo, tranquilo!" Colon was telling us to chill out. "Eight-nine-fiye-cero-wong-sis-wong-wong. I lib in 1878, Crotona Abenue."

Fake ass Mike Tyson looked at me like he wanted to say, "*I told your stupid ass this nigga speaks English.*" At that point, Colon got his handcuffs removed and walked over to an open cell where one of the R&D orderlies had a warm plate of rice and beans waiting for us.

"I know you're happy as shit now. *Bean and rice eating ma'fucka*," yelled the guy. Colon just turned around and continued stuffing his face.

"Jackson!"

"*I wonder if we're related?*" Mr. Jackson, who I came to know as CJ, was flirting with the attractive corrections officer.

Ms. Jackson didn't smile or anything. She switched her weight to her other leg, popped the gum she was chewing two quick times and rolled her eyes.

CJ got the picture. "Six-nine-nine-0-four-double-0-seven. 1331 Jefferson Avenue. *Brooklyn, ya heard!*" He ended his address with a smirk on his face. Ms. Jackson undid his cuffs and sent him on his way.

"Robinson!"

I already told y'all I was starving and sleepy. *A nigga like me didn't waste no time.* "895-zero-sixteen-twenty-seven. 1611 West 150th Street." As soon as I grabbed my plate, I was spooning shit into my mouth before I found me a seat on an empty bench. Shit, blacks are some bean and rice eating ma'fucka's too. Don't get it twisted. Just 'cause down south they be stuffing their faces with Hog Mog and shit don't mean we don't eat beans. We all the same anyway. Puerto Ricans, Dominicans and Cubans are just as black as we are. The only difference between a black and a Hispanic, in *my* opinion, *for most of us*, is the texture of our hair. Let me put it simpler, put us in a police line up and watch both of our asses get picked.

After we finished eating, things got quiet. Colon went back to sleep, on the floor of the holding pen this time, CJ was standing at the gate with his arms through the bars like he had done this many times before, and I was sitting there looking worried, thinking about my moms and my girlfriend, Charlene.

CJ turned to face me, extended his fist and said, "Niggas call me CJ."

I looked up at him and said to myself, "*Niggas should call you asshole,*" but instead I returned the gesture and kindly said, "Larry, but niggas in my hood call me 'L'." After my fist touched his, I guess he got tired of flirting with "*Big Butt*" because the *clown* took a seat next to me.

"Are your people's coming to get you out?" he asked as he kept his eyes glued to Ms. Jackson's rear end jiggling, as she walked by.

Again I wanted to say something to irk his ass like, "*Is the monkey that abandoned you coming to get your funny_looking ass?*" but I remained cool about the *twenty-one_questions* and as I looked over at Ms. Jackson who was now bending over I said, "I might not be getting out any time soon."

He looked at me, "Why not?"

I sighed and said, "I got a body", then my voice trailed off as Ms. Jackson walked by us again, "but I ain't do it though," I added.

"Me either," he said.

"I guess that makes two of us." I looked over at Colon and caught him scratching his butt through his filthy ass jeans.

"Did they find a weapon?"

I looked CJ in his face to see if he was genuinely concerned or just being nosy. I settled with him being concerned and I told him, "I don't know. I told you I ain't do it."

"Yo, lookie here, lil brah," I figured CJ to be about 40 years old or very close to it. Son was about 6'2" and about 200 pounds. "Them bodies ain't no joke. But at the same time, they're also easy to beat." He smiled, "A dead man can't tell no tales."

"But faggot ass, lying ass snitches, who probably want to get out of their own situations will." I relaxed my head against the wall, looked up in the air and sighed with a hint of frustration.

"Let me ask you something, young'n." CJ put on his big brother routine, so I played my position.

"*Shoot*," I told him.

He looked at me.

"Nah, not like that. I mean, kick it." I was beginning to relax now.

"How old are you?" he asked.

"Eighteen."

"You still go to school?"

"Just graduated."

"You got a girlfriend?"

"Several."

"Do you have one you can *trust*?" He sat a little more erect after he asked me that.

I noticed it so I looked at him, "My boo, Charlene, why?"

He relaxed himself, "Don't lose her."

"I'm not." I sat back against the wall.

"Don't push her away either. You said you got a homicide, right?"

I nodded my head. I was definitely trying to see what his point was in all of this.

"Well, you're going to be here at least two years fighting this thing. I just beat a body last year."

"*Go figure*," I thought.

"I laid up like thirty-two months before I beat them on a technicality. I lost my wife being hot headed though. She told me she wanted to go out to the club with her girlfriends one night. I was only in jail for like a month at that time, so I wasn't really trying to hear that ole girl wanted to party while I was pressing my rack. But I told her to go ahead and do her, and to be slick, I told her to go and find a nigga that'll tolerate that club hopping bullshit. The bitch called my bluff like a ma'fucka. I tried calling her the next day to apologize but I didn't get an answer. I kept calling for like a month straight, still the same fuckin' thing. Guess how I found out that she was done with me?"

"I know, the dude got knocked and y'all ended up in the same unit." *This nigga must think I'm new to this broad shit.*

"Nah, when that nigga was digging her guts out one afternoon, I guess she was trying to turn the ringer off and must've accidentally knocked the phone on the floor and off the hook. I heard this bitch telling some nigga his dick is like money, *guaranteed to keep her cumming.*"

I didn't want to laugh because dude looked hurt, but when he turned and looked at me I could tell he wanted to laugh too so I set if off. Ole boy joined me and that broke the ice, *so to speak.*

He was into his zone so he continued, "Don't fuck up like I did, young'n. Keep your broad. You're gonna need her. This shit is rough doing a bid by yourself. Ain't nothing like a lil visit here and there, some mail, a few flics from those who love you. Mind you, I said those who love you, not those who *you* got love for. There's a difference."

"No doubt."

"Got any kids?"

45

"Nah," I said.

"I thought that all you young niggas had babies all over the place."

"*Wrong young nigga.* I'm trying to play ball. I'm trying to get this scholarship to North Carolina. I need this break."

CJ looked at me. This time he stared as if he were studying me. "*I hope this nigga ain't gay,*" I thought.

"I believe you, son."

He used the word "*son*" more like a father figure would as opposed to a homie, so I took it that way and asked him, "You believe what?"

"I believe you ain't kill nobody."

I didn't need his opinion. "I told you that already," I said.

"Do you know who did it?"

"Yeah, but I ain't telling."

"Why not?"

Fuck he mean why not? I ain't no snitch. "Fuck you mean why not?"

"Why not? Why won't you tell on the person who really committed the crime you're charged with? That sounds crazy to take the weight for someone when your life is at stake here."

"'Cause," I was beginning to feel uncomfortable now.

"Because what? Give me your reason. Convince me because I'm missing something here and I know it."

"Because it's the *code of the streets*! That's why!" I was on my feet now.

CJ thought to himself, "*I guess some people still abide by the code.*" With that he got up, motioned for Ms. Jackson and when Ms. Jackson opened up the cell and just let him walk out, that shit bugged me out. But what happened next is something I'll never forget. CJ walked out of the cell, kissed Ms. Jackson square on the mouth, then looked back at me.

The nigga pulled his badge from his pocket, placed it around his neck, called Ms. Jackson *"Honey"* and told her that he'd see her in the morning. Before he left in the unmarked patrol car that sat outside waiting in the cut for him to return, he turned, looked at me again and said, "If you won't tell us who killed Louis Gonzalez, I hope you're attorney can convince a jury the way you convinced me." With that said, Detective Corey Jackson shook his head and exited the building.

CHAPTER SIX!

fficer Carla Jiminez entered the interrogation room where Curtis had been questioned almost two hours earlier. He sat leaned over, with his arms crossed, resting on his knees and his head resting on his arms. People had been in and out of the room the last past couple of hours so Curtis didn't budge when the female officer entered.

Ms. Jiminez sat down opposite of Curtis, placed her hands quietly on the table that separated the two and cleared her throat.

Curtis looked up. Officer Jiminez stared at him intently, trying to read whatever it was that was on Curtis' mind. But it was going to be hard trying to figure this young man out, especially by looking at him. Curtis Martin had his poker face on and had the two of them been gambling against one another, Carla would have been scared to make her move.

When the officer didn't say anything, Curtis placed his head back into his lap.

"So what's it gonna be?" she asked. She gently bit down on her lip.

Curtis kept his head in his lap. "Is my lawyer here yet?"

"Apparently your attorney couldn't make it. He said he was attending a trial and wouldn't be here until after night court was over. It's 7 o'clock now so that gives you at least three more hours with us." She was looking at her watch that always read military time.

Curtis sighed and said, "Well, just let me know when he gets here."

Ms. Jiminez tried another approach. "Do you think that your mother could forgive you after causing her to spend ten years of her precious life in prison because of you?"

This caught his attention. Curtis looked up and said, "My moms ain't going to jail. Y'all only got me. Y'all know the drugs were mine and that she ain't have *shit* to do with it, so save that bullshit for the birds."

Carla Jiminez slid the arrest report over to Curtis so that he could examine the document for himself. He read where it said that his mom was charged as his codefendant for conspiracy. He also knew that a conspiracy was an automatic *ten years.* "Call your boss in here," he said.

Officer Jiminez jumped up and raced out the door. After a few moments she returned with Detective Steve Todd.

Steve sat in the seat that his subordinate had previously occupied. He looked over at Curtis and said, "Your mother shouldn't have been put through *this* much."

Curtis got right down to business. "Check this out. I'll give y'all my buyers, but they won't just deal with *anybody* and they know not to talk crazy over the phone. We're gonna have to set up like a buy and bust. Like how y'all did with me and Mel." Officer Jiminez stole a glance at Curtis and caught the devilish grin he had on his face. "But they don't give me any money up front. I fronts them, and they hit me with my cheddar when I bring them the next pack. It's been going on for a while like that so the operation runs smoothly now."

"How many of them are there?" The detective was smiling, but he wouldn't let it show on his face.

"It's three of them. They're like one little crew."

Steve Todd grabbed his pen and pad and positioned his hand to start writing. "What's their names? Give me their names?" He looked down at his paper.

"Slow down player. I don't know their *real* names. You know we all go by our *street* names."

"Well, what are their street names? And by the way, we never caught your street name."

"You'll soon find out," Curtis said to himself, but out loud he said, "Their names are *'H', 'K' and Dee.'*"

"What the hell," the detective chuckled, "you running an alphabet crew?" He laughed harder.

"You won't be laughing for long," Curtis again thought to himself.

"How do you contact them?" asked the detective.

"It's funny you asked. Y'all fucked up my plans for meeting up with them earlier. What I usually do is cop from Mel, do whatever it is that I have to do, then go and meet them."

Carla stepped up. "So they're still waiting on you now?" This time Ms. Jiminez couldn't maintain her anxiety. She had to speak up. She was trying to get promoted and this collar would surely help out.

Curtis looked at her wondering where she all of a sudden retrieved her voice from. He said, "Yup," then he smiled at her.

"Let's set it up then. Give us the location and we'll have our people set everything up like if it's you that's making the drop. But we'll surprise their asses, won't we?" said Carla looking over at her boss.

He nodded.

"I'll have to page them and put in my code to let them know that I'm on my way. They usually hit me right back on my pager telling me it's okay to come through. So if they hit me back, y'all can roll. If they don't, it'll be a waste of time to set up *y'all's* operation."

"Jiminez, go get his cell phone." Curtis could hear the smile in the detective's voice.

When Ms. Jiminez came back, she passed Curtis his phone and let him do his thing. Curtis punched in seven digits and waited for a second. The room was quiet so everyone heard when the three loud beeps sounded off after the single ring.

Ring...Beep...beep...beep!

Curtis entered his code, "*1-007-5-0-225-60-30.*" He pressed the pound button to insure the message got to his people as soon as possible.

Across the city in the borough that birthed Hip Hop, *Homicide, Killer* and *Danger* sat parked on their Yamaha Banshee 4-wheelers in the park of their housing development.

"Ayo, I love this project," said the 5'8" lanky fifteen-year-old. *Homicide's* name was self-explanatory. Aside from selling drugs all day long, Homicide *murdered* people for a living.

"Ain't no other project on this planet like Edenwald," retorted *Killer*. He, too, was a lanky, 5'8", fifteen-year-old. He was a little darker than *Homicide* was, and every time Homicide *murdered* somebody, Killer would be right beside him emptying his gun into the victim as well.

"*Yeah, the BX, nicknamed Cook Coke Shit. It should've been called Homicide Bronx, The Killer Bx or the Dangerous*

Boogie Down," Danger chimed in with a little more enthusiasm than his two buddies. Everyone thought the trio were brothers due to them hanging around one another all day, every day. It was also their exact same height and close facial resemblances that caused others to think that way. As far as *Danger* and *his* reputation, everyone knew that *he* had committed just as many killings as his two friends had done.

Homicide's pager sounded but Killer had it in his possession because earlier that day, the threesome were being pursued by the police and to confuse the authorities, the trio switched coats to camouflage their identities. *Sort of like a mix-up thing.*

Killer looked at the device and got quiet.

"What's up, homie? What's popping?" Homicide was referring to the page on his beeper.

"Yo, who the fuck is code #1?"

Homicide tried to snatch his pager away, but Killer pulled it from his reach.

"Gimme my shit, son!" Homicide yelled.

"Who is it, yo!?" Killer retorted once again.

"That's my cousin, nigga. *C-Murder.*"

"Yo, it's some more shit on here, son."

"What else do it say?"

"It says 1, *dash*, 007." Killer looked at Homicide for an explanation to the rest of the code.

"Yeah, that's cuzo, the double 0 seven means *beef,* go head," he told his homie to continue reading the message to him.

"Five *dash* 0," he looked at his homie again.

"That's the police, *nigga.*" Danger stopped in mid-pull of his marijuana cigarette. *It was time to be alert.*

"225."

"That's us, that's here. Two twenty-fifth, nigga, *our* block." Homicide had a look on his face like, *"Damn, nigga, you act like you ain't know."*

"Six 0."

"Sixty minutes, son. One hour is his E.T.A."

Danger looked at Homicide because he wanted his buddy to explain to him what the abbreviation meant.

"Expected time of arrival," said Homicide. He then looked back at Killer.

"Three, zero."

"Huh," Homicide and Danger said, *"Huh"* at the same time. Then Homicide mumbled to himself, *"Three, zero. What the...?"*

"Turn it upside down, Killer." *Danger* made this request. He knew what the code meant because he was the one who made it up.

Killer complied and said, "O, E?"

"That ain't an O, y'all. That's a D. *D, E.* He means pull out the Desert Eagles.

With that, the trio's faces lit up like Christmas lights. Homicide pulled out his cellular phone and paged his cousin back.

Back at the precinct, Ms. Carla Jiminez shouted, "They just returned our call. It says 10-4. I guess that means they're ready and waiting." She was looking at her boss and smiling through her eyes.

Back in the *Edenwald Projects*, Homicide started the engine on his bike first. Killer followed his homie's lead and Danger did the same.

Homicide revved his engine by pushing his thumb throttle, waited for the motor to simmer, grabbed the clutch, put the ATV in first gear and then pulled off. *Itchy and Scratchy* were right behind him. They all hit second gear at the same time, gave it some more gas, placed their right foot near the back brake lever and put the quad's in the air. *Moe, Larry and Curly* each had one of their knees in the seat while their other foot stayed near the back brake as they wheely'd through the projects on their way to the stash house where they kept an arsenal of artillery.

One Hour later ...

Creeping through the 225th Street drive at 5 m.p.h., Curtis' Ford Expedition rolled through with only its fog lights lit. That was a sign that he wasn't in the vehicle. Curtis hated using his fog lights, but warned his lil homies that if they ever saw his truck come through with the fog lights illuminated, that meant someone was scheming and to send his SUV to *Kingdom Come.*

Inside the large vehicle sat Detective Steve Todd, Officer Carla Jiminez and narcotics officers John Santos and Ernie Williams.

The quartet fought to see through the dark tint that blanketed Curtis' windows. The area where the drop was to take place seemed unusually clear for that time of day during the summer season.

A few leaves blew across the ground. It also didn't help ease the tension that hovered in the truck that some of the lights in the neighborhood seemed to be out as well.

But whenever *Homicide, Killer and Danger* rode through the projects on their four wheelers, the tenants *knew* something was up and they always made it inside of their apartments as fast as they could.

"You ready, lil homie?" Homicide was talking to the passenger on his bike.

"No doubt, big homie," replied Lil Hahmo. *Lil Hahmo* was twelve years old. Since the day he turned ten, Homicide had him under his wing.

"Are you ready, young'n?" Killer was talking to his sidekick.

"No doubt, Killer *The Cap Peeler*," replied Lil K.I. *Lil K.I.* was trained just like Lil Hahmo was. They were the two oldest of the triplets.

"B.G., *Baby Gangsta*, you good?" Danger was talking to the third and smallest triplet.

"If it ain't rough, it ain't right. Let's get it popping, big homie," said B.G.

The Ford Expedition came to a halt when the nails that were strategically placed in the street pierced all four tires of the heavy vehicle.

"*What the fuck?*" Steve Todd felt the tires deflate and knew that something was terribly wrong. Then he heard what sounded like a lawn mower come to life.

Homicide and Lil Hahmo came flying from behind one of the buildings closest to the driveway on their two side wheels. When the bike leveled off, the duo pulled up right beside the driver's side window.

Killer and Lil K.I. came from the other side of the street and positioned themselves on the opposite side of the SUV, but in an area where they wouldn't be in the line of fire of their compadres.

"*Say hello to my little friend*!" It was cliché, but Homicide didn't care. Them lil young niggas were from the hood so anything they said sounded gangsta. As soon as Homicide made the statement, he leaned over to the side and gave Lil Hahmo all the elbow room that he needed. Lil Hahmo opened up his Mosberg pump shot gun like an umbrella and emptied his entire 17 shot drum clip into the driver's side front and rear windows and gave whatever else he could to the weak ass windshield. The bullets ejected from Hahmo's rifle like he was shooting a semiautomatic handgun. Glass and brain matter were everywhere.

Killer sat on his bike with two Desert Eagles making the passenger side of the jeep *strip itself*. As the large handguns turned the once luxurious car into recycled metal, K.I.'s lil crazy ass was off the bike walking towards the vehicle firing his two cannons singing, "*I'm from the Bronx, New York, things happen.*"

After the fireworks stopped, Danger and B.G. rode up with two containers of gasoline. The duo ran around the $40,000 heap of twisted metal and emptied the gas in and around the vehicle. B.G. jumped back onto the back of the bike where Danger patiently waited for him, looked at all of his homies who were ready to roll and yelled, "*Bllaaaapp! Bllaaaapp!*"

Danger lit his blunt, took a pull and tossed the match into the sport utility vehicle. The truck went up in flames and the *Dream Team* took off like *the fast and the furious*.

Back at the precinct in Queens, the police were beating the *dog shit* out of Curtis. Before going unconscious, Curtis looked up at the big brawny officers who were reenacting the Rodney King incident and mumbled, "*Code of the Streets, nigga*," then he fell out.

THE END!

Eight months after Larry was arrested, the murder case against him was dismissed due to the apprehension of the real perp.

Curtis died two days later at an area hospital. The press released a report that said he died of a heart attack. But a female nurse sent the original hospital report to Curtis' mom. The document showed that her son died as a result of the beating he took at the precinct. Ms. Martin took the report to Internal Affairs and an investigation has been underway ever since.

And Now
We bring you our feature presentation

UNWILLING
TO SUFFER

A Novel
by
Antoine Inch Thomas

DEDICATION

To everyone that has been through it,
this one's for you!

CHAPTER ONE

It had been three days since Daryl and I stood before a church full of our friends and family members and exchanged out lovely vows. My twenty-one-year-old ass, in my custom made wedding dress, was led down the isle by my father, who with tears in his eyes, *how sweet*, clutched my hand like it would kill him to let go. Once we reached the podium, the tune *Here Comes the Bride* abruptly ceased and I faced my soon-to-be gorgeous ass husband.

Daryl slowly lifted the see-through veil from my face as the Reverend Malcolm Cooper began his recital.

"Do you wish to take this woman, to be your lawfully wedded wife? To love and to cherish her? To protect and to care for? To administer and provide for? Through sickness and in health, till death do you part?" *I thought they only said that shit at white people's weddings.*

"I do," said Daryl, never moving his sexy eyes from mine.

"And do you," continued the reverend, "Take this man to be your lawfully wedded husband? To love and to cherish him? To protect and to care for? To administer and provide for? Through sickness and in health, till death do you part?" *And what about to fuck his ass night and day?*

"I do," I replied.

When all of our customary and personal vows were exchanged, Reverend Cooper looked over at my father, who passed my husband the ring and in conclusion said, "You may kiss the bride."

At that moment, oblivious to the tremendous cries of joy and applause that rose from our family and friends who packed the pews of the Harlem church, me, Mrs. Stephanie-Daryl-Manning, for the first time in my life, felt like I was in heaven. Because only an angel could make me feel the way Daryl did.

Three days later at out home in Mt. Vernon, New York, my and my other half lay snuggled together in our bed as we watched another re-run of the comedy sitcom *Martin*.

"Dee, do you think Gina and Martin are messing around behind the scenes?" I asked, referring to the lead characters on the television show. I ain't never like the name Daryl so I opted for calling his ass Dee.

"Probably Steph. They say there's a lot of infidelity going on in Hollywood. In fact, the rumor is actually that Martin and Pam are real life lovers," my husband said, also referring to a character on the show and calling me Steph for short.

"Nah uh, for real?" I asked sounding surprised as I leaned up on my elbows.

"Yup," said Daryl smiling seductively at me.

"What are you smiling at me like that for? You think you're slick. I know that look," I said, returning the sexy gaze. "You're trying to seduce me again," I added as I began unbuttoning my pajamas.

"Come here," said Daryl with his captivating charm.

Like the horny lil freak that I am, I slid over to Daryl's side of the bed and crawled underneath the covers. I made my way toward the foot of the bed, popped my head up from underneath the sheets and said, "Time to go snorkeling again. Be up for oxygen in five minutes." And as quickly as I popped my head up from underneath the blankets, I was back under again, taking Daryl into my warm ass mouth and massaging the underside of his penis with the wetness of my tongue.

"Ooooh!" moaned Daryl, he grabbed my head through the sheets and humped my face like he had done earlier that day. Feeling his legs tense up, I sucked harder and sped up my pace, swallowing everything he released. I continued my vigorous pace until Daryl once again became erect. I then released my grip and climbed on top of his ass taking control for my encore performance. After thirty minutes of intense lovemaking, I collapsed on my husband's chest and the two of us matched one another's breathing as we slipped into a realm of our own imaginations.

The vibration of Daryl's pager became a reality to me when I realized I was at home and not on a roller coaster ride at New Jersey's Six Flags like my dreams had been telling me. Raising my head to get a clearer tune-in of where the vibrations were coming from, I looked underneath our bed and noticed the red light flashing from my husband's Nike basketball shoe where his pager had been tucked. Retrieving it, I noticed that only one number appeared across the tiny screen and it had a code of 911 behind it.

Observing it I thought to myself, "Maybe it's one of his friends. I hope everything is alright. They usually don't call him this late at night, I wonder…" *Sounds stupid, doesn't it?*

Looking over at my husband who was sound asleep, *I* decided to return the call that seemed so urgent. I picked up our cordless telephone, strolled over to the bathroom in the hallway of our home and quietly sat on the toilet to relieve myself of my full bladder. Dialing the number, the telephone buzzed and was answered after the first ring.

Ring...

"Hello," said an unfamiliar voice that was soft and feminine.

"Somebody paged a pager?" I asked suspiciously.

"Bitch, don't be calling my goddamn house!" screamed the voice annoyingly through the telephone.

Click!

"Uh uh. No this bitch didn't," I said, redialing the number. *Fuck she think she is?*

Ring...

"Hello!" shouted the unfamiliar voice once again. This time with a bit of frustration.

"Listen here, Miss Thang, I don't know who the hell you think you're talking to but *you're* the one who..."

Click! She hung up again. Like she's *gangsta*.

Fed up, I placed the telephone on the bathroom sink and wiped myself clean. After flushing, I washed my hands and proceeded back into the bedroom where my husband lay sleeping, unaware of what had just transpired.

"Dee!...Dee!" I bellowed Daryl's name as I neared his comatosed ass.

"Huh," he said as he lay still like an incoherent toddler preoccupied with a novelty.

"Who the fuck is this bitch calling your pager at two o'clock in the damn morning?" I screamed. "Hello!" I continued as I aimed his pager toward his direction while simultaneously pressing the button that exposed the numbers.

"What! Calling who?" said Daryl trying to focus as the hallway light dimly lit the room.

"Your damn pager, nigga! Look at me would you!" I continued. *This nigga and that bitch had me mad as hell.*

Daryl rolled over and bewilderedly asked, "What the hell are you talking about, Steph? You're tripping right now. I don't have any idea who the fuck is calling *my pager* because *I* didn't answer the shit, did I, Steph?" His vulgar words crudely left his mouth and were unexpectedly received by my ass.

"Did you answer the shit?" As I spoke, I raised my voice an octave, *Whitney,* lowered it, *Mariah,* then mellowed it out to an even tone, *Lauryn Hill.* "Motha fucka, we just got married three fucking days ago and you got some bitch calling your damn pager at two o'clock in the fuckin' morning." I was standing over our bed with my hands on my waist clearly upset.

Daryl sat up on his elbows, asked me a stupid ass question and then answered it for me. "How did you know it was a female anyway? It could've been one of my boys. You know you're always assuming shit, Stephanie."

"Because I called the bitch back! That's how I know." I was staring at Daryl with lunacy and hysteria in my eyes.

"Hold up, hold up," said Daryl, getting out of our bed. "You checking my pager and shit now? Since when you started snooping around in a nigga's shit, Steph?" he asked, raising his voice.

As he placed his feet on the floor, I dropped my hands from my hips, raised them again, then continued my lecture like if I was Farra Khan or somebody.

"You my husband, ain't you? So I'll check the crack of yo ass if I wanted to," I said, rolling my eyes and wiggling my neck.

"What!" said Daryl, getting up. Daryl stood up because he felt he was the man of the house. As far as he was concerned, no one could tell him anything, not even me. At that point, his next reaction was an act of instinct.

Smack!!!

As we say in the 'hood,' Daryl slapped the shit out of me with the back of his hand like a pimp would do when one of his whores wasn't acting right. As I stumbled in surprise, my own reflexes compelled me to bounce back up and charge Daryl, striking him at the center of his nose.

Daryl screamed, "You fuckin' bitch!" He grabbed me by my shoulder length hair and swung me onto the bed, immediately jumping on top of me and sat on my chest. He then proceeded to strike me with three quick jabs to my face and head. *'Bong, bong, bong!'* "Calm your stupid ass down! What the fuck is wrong with you swinging on me like that? You crazy? Are you crazy, Steph?" he angrily asked. By this time, his irrational mind was on the verge of unbalanced psychosis and he didn't even realize that it was he who struck me first. *Fake ass Mike Tyson.*

"Just get off of me!" I screamed, as blood, tears and my nasal mucus mixed in together giving my face a nasty mask.

Daryl climbed off of me and allowed me to run into the bathroom where I remained for the next few minutes. He picked up his pager and examined the lone phone number that appeared on its screen. After erasing the familiar digits, Daryl sat down on the edge of the bed and looked down the hallway toward the bathroom. Fixing his face as if he were upset, he calmly yelled, "You ahight, Steph?" He paused for a second, looking for a response. When he didn't immediately receive one, he tried again. "I ain't mean to hit you. I just bugged out for a quick second…Stephanie? Steph!" Nervous that I may have collapsed, Daryl began walking toward the bathroom door. "Steph!" He continued to shout my name out frantically.

"I'm using the bathroom. Leave me the fuck alone," I said calmly. Then I flushed the toilet. *I should've threw my piss in his face.*

"Fuck it then," said Daryl, walking back to the bedroom. He began putting on his clothes and shoes, and once he was fully dressed, he grabbed his key ring and said, "I'm going out for some air. I'll holla at you when you calm the fuck down."

I heard the door slam telling me that it was okay to release the hollering I'd been holding in ever since the tears began flowing.

I cried frantically at first, then I calmed down. I stepped out of the bathroom and walked over to the window just in time to see Daryl bend the corner in his cherry red Land Rover. My premonition told me that he'd be gone at least until the morning, so I dropped down on the bed and buried my head into the pillow. I cried and cried until my head began hurting, then I rolled over and went to sleep.

Before I slipped into my state of unconsciousness, I thought to myself, "I hope I don't have to put up with this stupid shit for the rest of my life." *Don't we all ask ourselves that same dumb ass question?*

CHAPTER TWO

Experiencing an emotional hangover the following morning, I forced myself out of bed to locate and answer my ringing cordless telephone that I had flung across my room the night before. Waking up after the second ring, I tossed the covers off of my face and glanced at the clock. I spoke quietly to myself, "Damn, it's 6:30 in the morning. Shit! Why do people always seem to call at inappropriate times?" After the fourth ring, I realized that Daryl wasn't there to answer it either so I looked around, jumped off my quilted mattress and retrieved the telephone from a pile of unwashed clothing.

Ring...Ring...Ring...Ring!

Shaking the hair from my face, I answered the phone in a professional manner. "Good morning, Manning residence, Stephanie speaking." As quickly as the name Manning slid from my mouth, it hit me just like Daryl's punk ass did the night before and my ass became angry almost just as fast.

The deep voice on the other end of the telephone instantly startled me. "Yo, Steph." Daryl called my name in a tone that was symbolic and a reminder of the many good times we shared together, *mostly in bed.*

Pausing for only a few seconds, Daryl's voice seemed too irresistible to avoid. The love for the man of my dreams caused me to surrender easily as if nothing ever happened. "What, Daryl," I said, pushing my hair away from my face and glancing in the mirror. My face mildly stung from the episode the night before but no bruises had appeared. A half smile also crept from my beautiful ass face and Daryl knew it.

His next statement was, "I love you." *Damn, I couldn't hold out any longer.* The words that captured my heart after me and my husband's third date were repeated once again, reminding myself how much I loved him. I began to cry softly as Daryl continued to speak. "Listen, Boo, I'm sorry about last night. I shouldn't have reacted like that. You know I love you and would never hurt you." *Damn, I be acting like a lil bitch sometimes.*

"But you did!" I screamed, standing to my feet.

"Look, I know, I know. But will you please just listen to me for a second?" He paused, then called out my name. "Stephanie?"

Wiping my tears from my eyes and raising my eyebrows to express some attitude, I calmly answered, "I'm here."

"Damn, don't be scaring me like that," said Daryl nervously.

In my mind all I thought was, "Scaring you? Shiiit, you damn near frightened me to death. I should be the one petrified."

He continued, "Boo, I promise I won't ever put my hands on you again. I...I...I don't know what came over me," he said stuttering. Daryl was trying to formulate his story. "I think I bugged out on you because I love you so much and I can't stand the thought of losing you."

I immediately interrupted his ass. "If you love me so much, why do you have other bitches calling your pager?" I asked wanting the truth, but with any man, I'll only be told what he wants me to hear.

"Who? Monica? Monica is just some chick that Tommy recommended for a job. He thought we were hiring so he gave her my number and told her to give me a call."

"And the bitch is calling you at two o'clock in the fuckin' morning looking for a job? Nigga, please. The only job that bitch was interested in was a blow job," I said firmly.

Daryl tried to reason. "Steph, chill."

"No, fuck that!" I thought.

"Daryl, I'll speak to you later," I said matter-of-factly.

And Daryl replied like any lying man would, "Okay."

When Daryl pressed the 'End' button on his cellular phone, he thought to himself, "At least she's speaking to me. I'll just think of something that I could do to cheer her up. Maybe I'll pick her out some flowers and grab her some candy. She loved it when I used to do things like that." Then he thought, "Damn, I used to do a lot of cool, romantic shit when we first started dating. I need to step my game up and get back on my job before I lose her. Can't let wifey think that I don't love her anymore." After doing his personal analysis, Daryl started the engine on his truck and headed to work.

I pressed the power button on my telephone and figured I might as well stay awake. After scouring our untidy bedroom and recognizing the mess, I made up my mind to do some spring cleaning.

I didn't have a job because I didn't have to work. My husband made it clear that after we were married, I would quit my job as a bank manager and get used to being a housewife. We made plans to have three children together and we also looked forward to one day relocating south for retirement. *Picture that.*

Daryl was the General Foreman of a construction company he co-owned. His partner was an old Italian guy named Al Morro whom he met during an encounter at a coalition rally. Both men had the same form of ambition and the same goal: to work very hard and to one day own their own establishments. After the pep rally, the duo had dinner together. They exchanged telephone numbers that evening and they each ended up going home with a new friend, one another. Today, Mr. Morro, suffering from throat cancer, planned on selling his partner his share of the business for a fraction of its worth. With the money that Daryl planned on taking in, I had no reason to work. My job, according to Daryl, would be to become the best housewife in the world. *And I guess be the stupidest one too.*

Four years prior to our marriage, Daryl and I had become an item. We both knew one another from growing up in the same Brownsville, Brooklyn neighborhood, but the three year age difference, with Daryl being my senior, hindered him from approaching me sooner. He waited until he heard my high school was having its prom and that's when he made his move.

My school prom was scheduled for June but everyone learned about the date in May. That Mother's Day, Daryl, who was then twenty years old, approached me when he felt the time was perfect; at my church, in the presence of my parents. *Sneaky fuck.*

He entered the house of worship right when the community pastor was concluding his sermon. Daryl scanned the rows of the Lord's house until he spotted me and my family. He slowly crept up to the pew that was occupied by my family and kindly found a seat in between Mr. Johnson, my father, and myself. He knew me and my dad had a very good relationship. He also knew about the crush I had on his fine ass.

One day, on his way home from work, he spotted me conversing with a small group of my female friends. As he approached our small crowd with intentions of flirting, he overheard one of my friends in the group say, "Aye, Kee Kee," to one of my other friends in the group that Daryl also knew. "You know Stephanie likes Daryl, right?" Daryl heard his name and immediately ducked under the canopy of a nearby building. He remained out of sight but close enough to hear everything that was said.

Crossing her arms, Kee Kee shot back, "What Daryl?... Dee Manning?"

"Yup," replied the first girl rolling her eyes and switching her weight to her other leg. "Tell em, Steph!" continued the girl giving me a look that said, *"Bitch, don't act shy now."*

Shrugging my shoulders like a small child would do when they don't know the answer to a question, I added a smile to my face and said, "I'm in love with his fine ass. But he doesn't even notice me," I said, turning my huge smile into a frown.

Then my friend Kee Kee interrupted. "Or these," she said, tapping me on the underside of my fully-developed D cup breasts, giving them a gentle lift. Her action and comment caused all the young ladies to burst out in laughter.

It also caused Daryl to peek out of his hiding place and sneak a glance at an area of my body that he would soon get to know better, *literally.*

Daryl waited for us to leave before he decided to continue

on down to his own house. It was at that moment that Daryl began formulating his plan to one day make me his wife.

Back at the church, Daryl gave his friendly salutations to my parents and flirtingly kissed me on my ring finger before he was offered a seat. *I always knew he was up to something.* A few moments later, the service was over and everyone began making their way toward the exit. In the lobby of the church, my father, my mother and myself were all very surprised but happy about Daryl's attendance at our church. We surrounded Daryl and began our third degree questioning.

Mr. Jefferey Johnson, a well-mannered man standing 5'7" with a thin build, cocoa complexion and still looking good to be in his mid-forties, reached his hand out to give Daryl a handshake. Feeling the response was genuine, my father asked Daryl a serious question. "Young man, what brings you here to the Lord's house today? I'm just curious because I've never seen you here before. I was beginning to wonder if something tragic happened to someone close to you which turned you in this direction." My father peered into Daryl's eyes and patiently waited for an answer.

Anticipating the question, Daryl amicably replied, "I came here to ask your permission on something, Mr. Johnson."

Confused, my father squinched up his face, lowered his jaw, then tilted his head and asked, "My permission?" He brought his conversation to a momentary halt, then started to speak again. "What is it that you'd like to ask me, Daryl?"

Daryl gazed at my mother, then he brought his eyes back to my father and, as he reached into his pocket, his eyes left the face of my father and found its way over to my honey brown eyes. He retrieved a 4-inch black velvet case, opened it and revealed a

1½ carat tennis bracelet. He affectionately asked, "Mr. Johnson, will you grant me permission to accompany your daughter to her high school prom if she doesn't already have a date?" Daryl practiced those words for a week after he found out through the grapevine that no one had asked me to the prom. He just knew he'd score with them.

As tears formed in the corners of my eyes from the shock and happiness, my dad looked at me and noticed how happy I seemed at that very moment. He too became emotional, but before he could answer, Daryl grabbed me and my dad by our hands and said, "I promise to have her home by midnight if it's okay with you and Mrs. Johnson here." Daryl nodded at my mom. He placed the bracelet on my wrist and submissively waited for a response.

My mother, Mrs. Betty Johnson, took the pleasure in answering and said, "Daryl, that was very, very sweet and respectable of you." She paused, smiled cordially, then continued. "I really appreciate and respect the way you approached us and I admire your mannerism. My husband and I have no problem with your request, Daryl, and if Stephanie here," my mother said looking at me, "has no problem with it due to any previous arrangements, you have our blessings."

Interrupting our family's emotional moment, my pops walked over to me and said, "Stephanie, would you like to say anything?" He said so as he stood beside me, hugging me and caressing my arm.

Daryl just stood there enjoying the moment. He sensed that at that moment, my heart was melting and reforming to match his. *My coochie got wet too.* He also knew that his approach would have an everlasting affect on me.

He stepped closer to me, grabbed me by both of my hands and began caressing them inside of his own, physically reassuring me that it was okay to speak.

The only thing that came out of my mouth was, "I would love to go to the prom with you, Daryl." My statement was said with a mixture of tears, joy, laughter, teenage love and embarrassment.

Daryl then hugged me and whispered into my ear. Softly, he said, "Listen, Steph, I presented you with that bracelet for Mother's Day for a reason." As I tried to free myself from Daryl's warm embrace to correct him that I wasn't a mother, only a precious child, Daryl grabbed and pulled me closer to him and said, "I know, Steph. But one day you will have children, and I'm praying that they'll be mine." He looked down at me and smiled.

I returned the smile and thought, "I think I'm in love with this man already." Then I looked at the bulge in his jeans.

CHAPTER THREE

After leaving work, my husband jumped on the Bronx River Parkway at Fordham Road and headed north towards Mt. Vernon. A few exits before his designated stop, Daryl pulled off the ramp at Gunhill Road. At the light, he spotted who he was looking for. It was a short Mexican guy who walked from car to car trying to sell single-stem and bushels of red roses. As the pint-sized immigrant neared Daryl's 4x4, Daryl dug into his pocket and retrieved his wallet. Unfolding it and seeing its contents instantly reminded him of why he was making the purchase in the first place.

A mini photo of him and I which was taken during a trip to the Rye Playland amusement park seemed to reach right out and touch him. Daryl grabbed a twenty dollar bill from his small wad of cash, lowered the passenger side window, turned down his radio and leaned over to get a closer look at the bootleg merchandise. The army green stems and raspberry red leaflets were physical confirmation that the product was official.

The four-foot Latino noticed the twenty dollar bill in Daryl's hand which caused him to crack a smile, revealing a mouth full of light-brown, tartar-encrusted teeth. The man grabbed one rose and in a heavy Spanish accent said, "One flower, one dollar."

Daryl looked at the bundle of exotic plants and figured there were more where they came from so he asked the salesman, "Will you give me two dozen for twenty dollars?"

Without erasing the huge smile off his face, the puny bud peddler simply repeated, "One flower, one dollar."

Daryl couldn't help himself. He softly chuckled at the thought of trying to run game on the Spanish guy who couldn't even comprehend his offer. He motioned with his hand for the man to retrieve more flowers while simultaneously asking him, "Give me twenty roses. ¡Veinte! ¡Veinte! ¡Dame Veinte!" said Daryl, requesting twenty roses in the man's native language.

Overjoyed with Daryl's purchase, the miniature man ran over to his floral stash and returned with a total of twenty-five roses. Smiling, he said, "For you, veinte y cinco. Twenty-five amigo. Muchos gracias, señor." He bowed to Daryl as if Daryl were a king and though the scene was comical to Daryl, the light had changed and traffic was backed up so Daryl drove off sharing the humor with himself.

The loud honking of horns snapped Daryl from the trance his spending spree had placed him in and the voices of people screaming at him alerted him to move on. Hearing one of the comments, Daryl looked into his rearview mirror, threw up his middle finger, then stepped on the gas and uttered to himself, "What the fuck does he mean by 'Move that piece of shit?' I paid 60 grand for this truck. If it's a piece of shit, then it's my piece of shit." He then made his way back onto the parkway.

When Daryl entered our apartment, he didn't smell the usual aroma of chow brewing. Instead, he was struck by the sensual smell of incense burning in the air. The perfume-like fragrance filled the air and gave our house a relaxed atmosphere. The candles that were strategically placed throughout the main floor of our home sent a wave of confusion through Daryl's groin. With the object of his behavior the last subject the two of us dealt with before his cowardly escape, Daryl's irrational suspicion led him to believe that I was perhaps practicing some form of witchcraft to punish him. Nervous, he darted up the steps screaming out my name. "Stephanie!" He yelled my name as he took the steps two at a time. "Stephanie!" Reaching the top of the steps, Daryl let out a sigh of relief as he encountered me relaxing comfortably in our bathtub reading a novel called *Flower's Bed.*

Unmoved by his antics, I calmly said, "Hey Daryl, I didn't hear you come in."

"Yeah, uh, I'm home," he muttered. "Hey, Steph, hold on a second." Daryl raced back down the steps.

Since my back faced the door, I leaned up from my liquid herbal blanket, turned to see what my husband was up to, twisted up my lips, then leaned back into my resting position. I had earlier set aside my harsh feelings toward my husband when I was doing my house cleaning. At one point during my early morning sanitizing, I came across a stack of old love letters that Daryl would write to me at the beginning of our relationship but had soon after stopped. Reminiscing on the sweet and romantic style he once possessed, I decided to forgive him and forget about the bogus story he had concocted the night before regarding the page from Monica.

Returning back upstairs with both of his hands behind his back, Daryl walked into the bathroom and knelt down beside the tub. We made eye contact, which caused me to reposition my relaxed pose because the seductive look Daryl was giving me caused a small tingle to occur in my vaginal area. Returning my sexy stare, I looked into the eyes of my Knight in Shining Armor and softly said, "Honey, what are you up to?"

The tone and calmness of my voice sent a shockwave through my husband's body and the licking of my lips sent a message to his brain telling it to notify his private area about an oncoming flow of blood.

Smiling now from ear to ear, Daryl cautiously spoke. "I'm not up to anything, darling, but I did bring you something."

My eyes grew wide as I was presented with a beautiful bouquet of red roses. And before I could further react to the sentimental gesture, Daryl pulled out a letter that he had previously written when he made his way back down to the main floor of our home. Opening the scribe and bringing his eyes to mine, Daryl began to recite the loving words that he had poured out on paper just moments ago.

"Stephanie, there is only one kind of love, but there are a thousand imitations." He paused for a moment, then continued, allowing the emotional words to set in. *"Honey, it is very important for me to express to you how much you mean to me. I'm fortunate to be able to come home to my lovely wife, hold you in my arms and gaze into your beautiful eyes."* As Daryl continued to read on, tears of joy flowed easily down my cheeks, dropping softly and quietly into my bath water. I subconsciously grabbed Daryl's fist and held onto it as it clutched the flowers he purchased for me. I began to gently caress his backhand and knuckles while the heartfelt words smoothly left his mouth. *"I know it is difficult for you as it is for me when we disagree on*

things, but life seems to be full of trials of this type and over-whelming tribulations which test our inner strength, and more importantly, our devotion and love for one another. After all, Steph, it is said that true love is boundless and immeasurable and overcomes all forms of adversity. In truth, if it is genuine, it will grow stronger with each assault upon its existence."

As the words that crept from Daryl's mouth entered my head and settled into my heart, without thinking, I reached out and grabbed my husband kissing him long and hard. Daryl responded and our tongues danced wildly in each other's mouth as I helped my man strip down to his nakedness. We made a mess as the exotic blends that were mixed in with my bath water splashed over the sides of the tub causing our hormones to heighten. Lodged in the large bathtub with me, Daryl grabbed me at my hips and raised my midsection to meet his salivating tongue. His erection told me that he was in need of possessing me, but he decided to wait until the foreplay was over.

As he caressed my breasts, he began licking his way down to my belly, twirling his tongue in and around my navel, then making his way to my soaked slit. He sank his tongue into my fuming core and I screamed at my initial climax. *"I love making up after a fight,"* I thought. His tongue found my clitoris and he went to work on it making me cum wildly. He insanely lapped away, building up one orgasm after another, allowing me to peak with rapidity.

His thumbs were parting my labia like the Red Sea, making it easier for his tongue to sink all the more deeply into my aching vagina. I felt his ears wriggling against my thighs as they clamped around his head. He sucked my clitoris repeatedly, sending an ecstatic desire flowing through me.

I hit the top of the rainbow and jerked convulsively. I grabbed his bald head, looked up at him and saw his face sodden with saliva and vaginal juices. Daryl then scrambled over top of me and let me feel his awesome hardness against my soaked and aching love nest.

Grabbing the underside of my knees, Daryl spread my thighs as far apart as possible, and with excellent precision, he slowly pushed the head of his manhood into me, causing me to gasp with pleasure. "I love you, Stephanie," he said to me affectionately.

"I love you too," I said with my eyes halfway open. I was still slightly delirious from the multiple orgasms I had from the oral play.

Daryl wiggled his hips violently as I felt his thickness invade me as it had never done before. Every other time we made love, it was either planned or gentle. This time, however, his lust seemed more aggressive. The soft, rustling sound of his dangling testicles slapping against my butt was driving me crazy.

Then I somewhat became the woman I was the night before. I caught eye contact with Daryl and in a deep, demented voice I screamed out, "Fuck me, Dee! Fuck me hard!" Catching him off guard caused him to surprisingly react. He ejected his manhood from my love tunnel, stood up and motioned me to step out of the bathtub.

Looking at his magic wand, then glancing back at his face, I saw Daryl's mouth moving and was entranced by the words that followed. "Bend over and grab your calves!" he said firmly. I complied as usual and as he entered me from behind, he grunted on the first stroke. He then rammed forward and stuffed every inch of his human sausage into the narrow confines of my tight little oven. Drilling in and out of me, he created a constant friction that tripped orgasm after orgasm.

Before we knew it, it was over. Daryl emptied everything he had into my drained and exhausted ass and we made our way to the bedroom. With just enough strength to go one more round, Daryl gave it to me one more glorious time in the missionary position to solidify his peace. The final round caused the two of us to sleep well into the next morning.

CHAPTER FOUR

T he next morning, Daryl was awakened by the sound of water running in the shower. He looked over at the clock and it read 11:17 a.m. Before he could overreact for being late for work, he remembered that it was Saturday, his day off.

Pausing to think about his next move, Daryl heard a beep that was all too familiar. His pager had gone off while I was in the shower. He retrieved the small tracking device and pressed the button that revealed the hidden digits. As he did so, his pager went off again. It was none other than Monica.

Monica is a woman that Daryl had met five weeks prior to our getting married. Because she resided in the area that his company had currently contracted, their relationship, which began as a casual one, naturally blossomed. As the weeks passed, the time they spent together increased, and so did their passion for one another. They went from platonic conversation to romantic French kissing. They eventually crossed the line. Monica knew about me, but she didn't care. She knew what Daryl was physically attracted to, and she possessed it.

During one of their intense conversations, Daryl expressed to Monica one of the physical attributes that he was attracted to in most women. He told her it was their behinds. Daryl was infatuated with women who possessed large rear ends and Monica's backside was just that.

A far cry from my physical stature, Monica was just as equally attractive because her buttocks were also just as big.

I'm almost as tall as Daryl is. My 5'8" voluptuous frame is encased in a golden brown honey nutshell. My breasts are huge and my thighs are thick like my ass. My body is nice and firm and, as a joke, Daryl would tell me that I am built like a brickhouse. My shoulder length hair is jet black and my deep brown eyes bring out my nicely groomed eyebrows. I have a small nose which compliments my beautiful smile and my high cheekbones make me always appear to be happy. I am a natural beauty and everything that Daryl ever wanted in a woman, *until he met Monica.*

Monica on the other hand is tiny in height, just three inches over five feet. She possesses a light complexion that surrounds her teal green eyes. She keeps her hair styled and cut short like R&B sensation Anita Baker which accentuates her flawless skin. Her breasts are average, and as Daryl would say, *"They are a handful."* She was also blessed with a small waist which in turn exaggerates the size of her butt. Her bottom half is built like a horse. She has large muscular calves and thighs, and according to her fling, *"the perfect butt."* Whenever Monica and Daryl make love, their sessions would always end in the doggy-style position. The way her backside would open up to invite him in as she lay perched up on her elbows, his erotic state would lure him to stroke uncontrollably, eventually causing him to erupt like a volcano dumping everything he has into her.

Daryl himself is a gorgeous fella. He's built like a warrior.

He stands 6'2" and his 200 pounds are all muscle. His smooth chocolate-colored tone looks edible to most women and he keeps his head shaved bald. Among other things, his three carat VVS cut diamond earring top off his sexiness.

Daryl is also very kind and respectful. He always holds doors open for women and he has no problem speaking to anyone. Daryl also dishes out money to panhandlers and his plans to one day start up a charity foundation for underprivileged children never deteriorated.

Daryl now had to act fast and figure out a way to return Monica's page without getting caught by my ass. Thinking quickly, Daryl walked over to the bathroom and peeked inside. He called out to me with the same tone he had used during our sexcapade. "Stephanie, sweetheart."

Getting wet almost instantly, I responded as I had done during our sexathon, playing along with Daryl's romance. Hoping that another round was in the works, I called back out to my hubby. "Yes, Dee." As a huge smile appeared across my face, Daryl began to speak.

"I'm gonna run and get us something to eat," he shouted.

I turned the water off and asked, "Where are you going, to McDonald's?"

"Nah, they stopped serving breakfast at like 11:30 a.m." Looking at his watch he continued, "It's like 11:40 a.m. right now so I'll run and grab us some lunch from somewhere else. Would you like anything specific, honey?" Daryl was almost dressed.

Thinking for a quick second, I shot back, "Just grab me a tuna fish sandwich on hero bread. And put lettuce and tomatoes on it." *That'll do for now. We'll do some gourmet shit another time.*

"Anything to drink?" he asked.

"Your thang," I said jokingly.

"What?"

"Nothing, I was just joking. Listen, I'll stir up some Kool-Aid while you're gone."

"Ahight. Love you, Steph," said Daryl closing the bathroom door. Daryl gargled with some mouthwash and spit it out into the kitchen sink.

"I love you too," I said turning back on my shower water and drowning in my thoughts as I rubbed myself. *"I love that man too much I think."*

Exiting our home, Daryl glanced up at our bedroom window to reassure himself that the coast was clear and that it was safe to make his next move. With an *'all clear'* sign posted in his head, Daryl flipped open his cellular phone and entered his sport utility vehicle. Unclipping the pager from his waistband to check yet another call from Monica, Daryl recognized the code and dialed her number.

7-1-8-5-5-5-3-5-8-4-0-0-2

Ring...Ring...Ring!

Monica threw on her sexy *come-sex-me* voice. "Hello."

"Yeah, what's up, Boo?" said Daryl nervously with a small touch of confidence.

"It took you long enough," continued Monica in her sexy tone.

"Yeah, I know, but you know," said Daryl, referring to me without mentioning my name.

"Whatever," she said, sucking her teeth.

"So what's up? When am I going to see you again?" asked

Daryl, hoping and silently praying to himself that their engagement would be postponed for a later date.

Demandingly, Monica said, "Now!"

"Now?" cried Daryl.

"Now! I want that big dick of yours now! And if you don't bring your ass over here right this second, you don't ever have to worry about hitting this anymore."

Click!

"*Damn!*" thought Daryl. "Now I have to make up an excuse for why I was gone so long." He spoke to himself as he continued in the direction of Monica's love haven.

Arriving at Monica's condo, Daryl pulled his truck into her two-car garage, exited his SUV and pressed the 'Down' button on her automatic garage door opener.

The door was unlocked to Monica's apartment and when Daryl entered, he peeked inside and called out her name. "Monica."

"In here," she said in her alluring voice.

Searching her home, Daryl found Monica lying on her bed covered in her silk robe. She was lying on her back, perched up on her elbows with one leg pointing at him and the other seductively raised at the knee. Her finger and toenails were painted the same color green as the robe she wore, and her mattress was also covered in satin sheets that matched the color of her sexy garment and nails. She removed her designer sunglasses revealing her summer green eyes which seemed to be a little too much for Daryl. He lost his composure a bit and began to unzip his pants when Monica interrupted him. She waved her pointer finger side to side indicating that she didn't want him to get undressed. She looked up at him and said, "Uh uh. Keep your pants on. I want you fully dressed. Now, come here!" She demanded his approach using her index finger for emphasis.

As Daryl neared his prey, his manhood stiffened at the sight of her unloosening her robe. Monica let the silk undergarment drop to the bed exposing a set of erect nipples and a hairy soaked mound. She dipped her finger inside of herself, pulled it back out and ordered her plaything to sample her goods. "Taste me, Daryl!" she commanded.

Without hesitating, Daryl licked Monica's finger like an adolescent would do a Popsicle on a hot summer day. Then, without asking, she undid his zipper, pulled out his magic stick, spread her legs like the Red Sea and laid back on her bed.

Daryl didn't have to be told anything else. He dove into her warm mitten, little head first and intensely pumped in and out of her for what seemed like ten minutes. They both climaxed simultaneously, and when Daryl was done, he collapsed on top of his beautiful love doll.

"Are we going to lay here all day?" she asked.

"Um, nah." He then realized that he was originally on a mission to retrieve some lunch for his wife. Checking for his pager, he assumed he had left it in his truck so he zipped up his pants and headed for the door. As he entered his jeep, Monica's door slammed and she yelled out, "Call me later!" That was his cue to get going.

On the way back home, Daryl stopped off at a Subway restaurant and purchased an 8" tuna fish sub with lettuce and tomatoes. He entered our premises five minutes after that and found me sitting in our living room watching a rerun of the comedy sitcom *Martin* with the volume on mute. In my hand was *Flower's Bed*, the novel I was reading the night before. *Damn, this book is good!*

With a half grin on his face, Daryl spoke up, "Hey, Steph." He looked around nervously, then continued, "Yo, it was crazy traffic out there. I'm sorry, honey, I tried to hurry up back."

Without looking at him, I calmly replied, "I'm not hungry anymore. I made myself a turkey bacon with lettuce and tomato sandwich a little while ago. I'm fine now."

Confused, Daryl didn't know what to say or do next. He managed to mumble. "So how's that book? Is it any good?"

"Um hm," was my only reply.

Feeling like the time was right, Daryl snuck into our first floor bathroom and began washing off his penis. When he looked up to retrieve a towel, he noticed me at the door looking at his limp member through the mirror. I slammed the door as I walked out causing Daryl to run behind me.

"Steph!" he yelled as she darted up the stairs. "I caught my thing in my zipper and I was just wiping if off...fuck!"

I slammed our bedroom door in his face, striking him in the nose. The same feeling had come over him which he experienced when I struck him in the nose a few days prior.

Daryl flung open the door and tried to hug me as I jumped on the bed to hide my tears. We struggled and I began to swing my arms wildly to keep my unfaithful husband away from me. Daryl, being a bit stronger than me, grabbed me by my hair hoping that it would calm my ass down. The tugging of my hair only added fuel to the already burning fire. "Stephanie, calm your ass down! Fuck!" he yelled over his heavy breathing.

I didn't comply. In fact, as soon as I spotted a clear shot, I took it.

Boom! I punched his ass right in the nuts.

As the pain eased its way up to Daryl's stomach, he dove on me, pulled my head back by my hair and rammed my shit several times into the mattress. On the last shove, he momentarily held my head down hoping to pacify my anger.

"I said stop flipping right!…Huh!…You hear me woman? I will beat your *motha fuckin'* ass up in here if you keep attacking me like you're crazy." *All he needed to do was inhale some helium, and talk with a lisp. He'd be Mike Tyson for sure then.*

For a moment, I wouldn't move. Then I spotted my cordless telephone and went for it.

"Oh, you trying to call the cops on me? Hell, nah, bitch," yelled Daryl, knocking the phone to the floor.

All I could do now was let out a loud cry. "Aaaagghh!"

Daryl released me and said, "Fuck you then!" He eased his way off of me nice and slowly. The clock that sat on the end table was the next closest thing to me and when Daryl saw me lunge for it, he ran out of the room only to hear me yell, "You the bitch nigga! I hate you!" I then proceeded to cry.

Daryl made his way out of the house and did what he had become accustomed to doing – he ran to his mistress.

I found the telephone, picked it up and pressed speed dial. Ring…ring!

"Hello," said a female voice cordially.

"I fucking hate him!" I screamed as my tears dripped down my face.

"You know what, girl, I'm on my way over there right now," said my childhood friend Kee Kee. "I knew you shouldn't have married that sorry ass nigga in the first place." Kee Kee continued on with her rambling as she searched for her keys.

I laid the telephone beside me and pressed the power button ending the desperate call. I laid in my bed crying until my close friend arrived.

By this time, Daryl was across town lying in bed with Monica. As he lay under the covers, Monica sucked his manhood to erectness and once he stood at attention, she eased herself on top of him. She spoke in a mocking voice as she rode him. "Awww, Mommy gonna take care of her baby," said Monica screwing up her lips.

As she humped him, he laid still as if her love box had no effect on him, but after the first minute or so, the two of them began humping in sync with one another.

Daryl thought to himself, *"Fuck it, at least I got one bitch that's going to act right."*

On the other hand, Monica had something else in mind. She thought, *"He'll be mine. I just have to have a little more patience."*

On the way over to lend me some support, Kee Kee thought about her own past and the drama that she herself had been through.

Growing up, all of Kesha's family was very close. Cookouts almost every weekend, small family reunions every couple of months, the kids would even have slumber parties over whoever's house had the most food.

One time when Kesha was about 11 years old, she and one of her female cousins, who was 13 at the time, decided to play house. Her 13-year-old cousin, Charlene, who had more experience with life, was chosen to be the daddy while Kesha accepted the position of mommy.

"Kee Kee! Get your butt in this house and clean this place up!" Charlene demanded. Their play house was Charlene's bedroom.

As Kee Kee picked up the clothes that were scattered about the tiny bedroom, she fussed to her play husband, pretending to be mad about the whole cleaning situation.

"Charles, I'm tired of cleaning up after you." The two felt that Charles was the closest boy name to Charlene so whenever they played house, Charlene was referred to as Charles. Kee Kee paced the room, picking up any and everything that she could find.

When she mistakenly overlooked a grey tube sock that her foot had been covering, Charlene noticed it and played her role as the mean husband.

"Kee Kee!" she yelled from her position on the bed. Charlene was on her knees in an upright position. "You missed a dag on sock, stupid. You know that that's gonna be your butt now."

Kee Kee glanced down, looked at the sock, and when she tried to reach down and pick it up, Charlene was already on her. The two girls went at it like kids usually go at it when they're playing, but Charlene was a little too rough, and what was supposed to be a soft body slam, ended up being a semi pro wrestling technique.

Kee Kee slipped and bumped her private area on the bed's headboard. She screamed in agonizing pain which scared Charlene for a second. But Charlene was the older cousin, and had to take charge of the situation.

"Kee Kee, let me see where it hurts." Charlene was standing in the middle of the room.

Kee Kee pointed.

Charlene walked over to the bedroom door, made sure that

it was secure, turned around, then said, "Kee Kee, I need to look at it. Let me make sure you're okay."

That was the same line used on Charlene three years prior to that incident from another older cousin, this one was a male though. The next thing you know, every chance that Charlene got, she was checking to make sure that Kee Kee was okay. Kee Kee never said a word to anyone. She never enjoyed it either. Then one day when she was about 17 years old and a little tipsy from drinking, the hookey party at Mary Sue's house that was occupied by only one black person, herself, got a little crazy.

The six girls were playing Truth and Dare. When the bottle spun around to Jennie, a 16-year-old petite little thing with blond hair and blue eyes, she chose the dare.

The other four white girls huddled up together, leaving Kee Kee and Jennie to wonder. Then Kate, the older and more aggressive one of the bunch turned to Jennie and said, "We dare you to kiss Kesha on her coochie." The girls looked at each other and giggled. At one time or another, all of the five white girls had kissed and touched one another in forbidden taboo ways. It was a first and a big hype to perform on the black girl, Kee Kee.

Jennie was cheered on, and with a mixture of bourbon and a whole lot of pride, Kee Kee laid back and let the *Brady Bunch* take charge. After about ten minutes, Kee Kee's leg started to wiggle. Her panting turned into moans and her slow steady breathing increased in speed. The next thing you know, Kee Kee experienced her first orgasm. And like a crackhead with his first hit of the pipe, or a dope fiend's first bag of boy, Kee Kee continually looked for that special high from both men and women alike. Whoever could produce, she was the ever-willing recipient.

But now none of that mattered. What mattered was that I was hurting and needed some support. Kee Kee knew that I was strictly dickly, so she never disrespected me. Now I needed a shoulder to lean on and Kee Kee would always be there to hold me down.

CHAPTER FIVE

JIMMY'S CAFÉ, THE BRONX ...

Daryl and his coworkers took their lunch break thirty minutes late because the deadline to reopen the exit ramp at Fordham Road on the Major Deegan Expressway was at 12 noon. All morning the twenty man crew worked feverishly and effectively as they laid down coat after coat of generic cement and tar. The large, expensive concrete mixer truck spun while Daryl and his team did an excellent job of leveling off the damaged pavement.

Forty-five minutes after eleven, 'M & M Construction' called it a wrap and took a break as the first twenty some odd cars tested the freshly laid limestone.

The hungry and exhausted gang of black and Hispanic men filed into the exotic restaurant and filled a row of booths that lined the windows facing the highway. The men gazed out the windows reminiscing on the work ethic that helped them complete the impressive project.

Tucked into a booth were Daryl and his close friend, Thomas Philips. Thomas and Daryl worked together on every job for the past three years and from the beginning, Daryl began noticing a lot of similarities between the two. Thomas was short and stocky and kept his hair cut short. The duo would have lunch together almost all of the time and would talk about everything they wanted out of life. Thomas soon became Daryl's confidant, and whenever the issue about women would come up, Thomas was always willing to put in his two cents.

Thomas looked over at his boss' plate and asked, "What do you get out of eating cottage cheese?" Pointing, he continued, "I just don't get it. All it is is spoiled milk." He leaned back and rested his hands on his lap.

Daryl scraped the last two spoonfuls into his mouth, dabbed the corners of his lips with his napkin and simply replied, "I like it. Tommy," he asked calmly, "aren't there some things that you like that people don't seem to understand?" He looked at his friend and swallowed the last of his food.

Thomas leaned forward, placed his hand on his chin, moved his eyes side to side as if he were thinking and serenely said, "No. You see, Daryl, you're different."

"I'm different?" Daryl interrupted. He too leaned forward, indicating that he was interested in what his friend had to say.

"Daryl."

"Stop calling me Daryl, Tommy. I hate that name. You remind me of my mother when you say Daryl like that."

"Ahight, ahight. Anyway, Dee, how can you cheat on a wonderful girl like Stephanie?" Demonstrating by counting on his fingers, Thomas continued, "I mean, come on now, the girl has class, she's friendly, she's smart, has a great sense of humor, she puts up with your bullshit and, to top it all off, if you don't mind me saying, the girl is fine as hell," said Tommy, holding up six of his fingers.

Daryl reached for his ice water, took a sip through his straw and said, "I don't know, Tommy. I don't even know. I mean, you're right. All that stuff you just said about Steph is absolutely true. I love her to death too, Tommy. And I would never, ever leave her for another woman, but for some strange reason, other women look good to me too." Looking his friend in the eyes, Daryl continued. "Tommy, Stephanie is a dime in her own right, but other chicks be dimes in other ways and, for whatever reason, I can't seem to help myself." Noticing the dismal look Tommy was giving him, Daryl ended his poor excuse for an explanation, and with a look of bewilderment himself, he asked, "What, Tommy? Why the crazy look?"

Thomas shook his head, slowly raised up from his seat and said, "Dee, I see attractive women all the time too and do I wish I could sample what's in their panties? Sure I do. But, I know it's just a feeling that will soon pass. Once the woman is out of my sight, the lust is gone right along with her. Dee, you have to realize what it is that you have at home. You need to stop thinking with your little head and give the big head a chance to reason," he said tapping his temple. "Before you know it, your wife will get fed up. All the pain and suffering you placed upon that woman's shoulders will be too much for her to bear and she will without a doubt leave your ass. Trust me on that one," said Tommy pointing a finger at Daryl.

"Boss!" yelled one of Daryl's workers from a nearby table. "Two minutes!"

"Ahight," replied Daryl, waving his hand.

All the guys began finishing up their lunches while Daryl sat alone thinking to himself. Thomas laid a five dollar bill on the table and removed himself from the booth. Daryl thought, "What the fuck am I doing? I'm playing myself right now." After a few more minutes, he too got up and left the restaurant.

Daryl attributed most of his bad behavior to his lack of family. Although his cousins Cynthia and Sharon were present in his life, it wasn't the same anymore without his mother, father and older sister.

When Daryl was growing up, he and his sister Donna, who was three years his senior, were the best of friends. Years ago when Daryl was just a toddler and Donna was six years old, Daryl wandered off by himself and ventured into a nearby housing project. A butterfly of remarkable size and color is what had his attention. It's what led him on his temporary journey.

Donna looked up when she heard her mother screaming out their names. "Donna! Daryl!"

Mrs. Patricia Manning was 26 years old. Her clear skin was dark, but she was still one of the most beautiful women in her neighborhood. She was also petite, and her vigorous workouts kept her body nice and firm.

With her pocketbook hugging her shoulder like a gun holster, Mrs. Manning continued to scream out frantically for her son and daughter. "Daryl! Donna!"

By now, Donna was on the verge of pissing her pants because she too was looking for Daryl, who was supposed to be by *her* side at all times.

Donna was scared. She knew that it was *her* fault that Daryl was missing. She knew that she had no business playing *'Double Dutch'* on the opposite side of the park where she was told *not* to go.

When Daryl wasn't anywhere in sight, Donna decided to

cross the street and trek through the notorious Marcy Projects, now known for raising rap veterans like Jay-Z, Memphis Bleek and Sauce Money.

Donna poked her head into every building and checked every elevator and stairwell. She went inside of every local grocery store and she even checked the parks in the projects. Finally she got tired. As soon as she was about to give up and accept her ass whipping, Daryl appeared out of nowhere.

"Donna! Donna!" he yelled. "Look what I got." Dressed in a powder blue Lee jean suit, three-year-old Daryl wobbled his way into Donna's presence holding the butterfly by its wings with both his thumbs and index fingers.

Donna had her hands at her sides, her bottom lip poked out and she had dry tears on her cheeks. When Daryl noticed that his sister looked as though she had been crying, he raised his hands, nudged the colorful insect in her direction and said, "Donna, look what I got for you. I caught it, and I want you to have it." He was pushing it towards her face.

Donna was upset at first, frightened even. She knew that if she lost her little brother that their mom would kill her. But Daryl looked so cute. His innocent eyes told his sister not to worry, that everything was okay. Donna grabbed Daryl, hugged him, kissed him on the cheek, grabbed him by his wrist and led him back to their mother.

"Where the hell have you two been?" cried Mrs. Manning as the duo approached.

Daryl held the butterfly up so that their mother could see it, while Donna spoke, "Mommy, please don't be mad at us. You always buy us nice things and we just wanted to give you something back." For a six-year-old, Donna was incredibly smart.

She paused to let her statement sink in, knowing that it would surprise and calm her mother. Then she continued, "Daryl and I caught this butterfly for you and we wanted to surprise you with it. That's why we didn't come out until you stopped screaming. You looked mad and we thought this would make you happy. Right, Daryl?"

Donna looked down at Daryl and nudged him. All he did was nod his head and say, "Um hm."

That's all it took. Mrs. Manning was satisfied and the children were relieved. At least Donna was. Daryl didn't quite understand what part he played in the whole situation, but it was all good though because for the next seven years, Donna and Daryl looked out for one another just the same.

It wasn't until almost a decade later that Daryl experienced his first real nightmare.

Daryl's Aunt Carol, who was his mother's youngest sister, had finally succumbed to breast cancer, which she fought hard for years to beat. On the way to the funeral home, upon request of Daryl's father, Little Daryl was to ride with his cousins in their limousine because every time he saw his mother sobbing, he would get scared and begin crying hysterically right along with her.

Dark clouds covered the sky on that gloomy afternoon as rain blanketed the half empty streets. A power line was struck along their route which caused the stop lights on their path to short out. Daryl's sister and parents never even felt it when the truck hit them. The driver of the 18 wheeler, who was intoxicated out of his mind, later told police that he thought their vehicle was a large puddle of water, and that he wanted to see it splash all over the place. It was *his* insane reason for doing 70 mph in a

35 mph zone. He also stated that the reason he kept going was because the puddle didn't splash all over the place like he wanted it to. That it stayed stuck to the front of his truck. Then he felt himself being pulled from his rig onto the street. There he was pounced on until the police and the ambulance arrived.

At trial, the truck driver was found guilty of Driving While Intoxicated and involuntary vehicular manslaughter. He was subsequently sentenced to three years probation. The driver was white and his father was a United States senator.

A month after the trail, a trust fund was mysteriously set up for Daryl and $150,000 was deposited into the account. 50,000 for each body. To the senator, that's what Daryl's parents and older sister were worth. He was up for reelection at the end of the year and he felt he was in need of doing a good deed. Needless to say, one week before the election the senator choked on a chicken bone while eating dinner at home with his mistress, another male senator.

Eight years later, when Daryl turned 18, the $150,000 had doubled leaving Daryl $300,000 to use as a down payment for a partnership at M&M Construction.

CHAPTER SIX

R ing...ring...ring!

"Hello," I answered.

Daryl waited for a second. After contemplating his approach, he decided to speak. "Stephanie."

I removed my earring and switched the telephone from one ear to the other. The rumbling made Daryl think that I was going to hang up on him. Nervous, he yelled out, "Steph! Wait! Please don't hang up!"

I rolled my eyes and coldly said, "What Daryl?"

"We need to talk, Steph."

"About what?" I shot back, while maintaining my reserved attitude.

"Can we talk face to face? Steph, I want you to look into my eyes and see the sincerity for yourself when I tell you what I have to tell you." *Niggas always say that shit.*

"Daryl, I am tired of your shit." Daryl knew whenever I called him Daryl instead of Dee that I was truly upset with him. He realized that his promiscuous behavior was destroying our marriage, so, in an effort to fix the problem, he figured reestablishing his trust with me was a top priority. Daryl had no real attachments to Monica. Their relationship was based solely on sex and the loving wasn't good enough to leave me for. As far as Daryl was concerned, if Monica didn't have a problem sleeping with married men, she had to have more on reserve. And relieving herself of one of them shouldn't be a problem.

"Listen," said Daryl pleading. "I know things have been messed up between us lately and…and…and I know you know I love you. Please, Steph, just give me a chance to explain. Hear me out at least." Daryl was nervous. He always stuttered when he was nervous.

"I'm listening," I said, asking myself what harm would it be in hearing the man out. *Stupid me.*

"Steph, I'm all smelly and stuff. I haven't been home to change or wash up in days and I've been working everyday in the same filthy underwear. I've been at Tommy's house all this time." Daryl made sure he added that in to make him still seem innocent. Prior to this phone call, he spoke to Tommy and explained to him that if I called to verify his whereabouts, that he'd better keep the story tight. He continued, "I promise I'll be in and out of the shower, and as soon as we're done talking, I'll grab some things and leave, if you want me to."

I remembered the words that my friend Kee Kee drilled into my head a couple of days ago. It seemed to echo as I recollected on the verbal warnings. *"Steph, the nigga ain't shit. If you take his ass back this time, he'll keep doing you wrong. And don't believe a word he says. Trust me, girl, everything that comes out of his mouth at this point must be considered a lie. Because in his situation, he'll say anything to make it right. And under no circumstances do you let him come back into your house. Not until he's completely out of your system."* I thought, "I'm grown. I can handle myself." *Yeah, right.*

FIFTEEN MINUTES LATER ...

"Mmmph, mmmph, mmmph, oooh, Daryl!" I said, moaning over my tears. Daryl had me in the missionary position with my legs wrapped around his waist. He stroked me aggressively as his words passionately left his mouth.

"Uh, uh, uh, oooh, Steph. I love you, Steph. I love you so much."

"I love you too, Daryl." Daryl pounded and pounded every inch of his manhood into me watching my eyes roll back into my head. Our intense lovemaking put me under emotional hypnosis and everything that Daryl said to me, my stupid ass believed.

Slamming his tongue into my mouth and observing my closed eyelids, Daryl knew he was in control. He loosened the grip my legs had around his waist, gripped me by the underside of my thighs forcing my knees to spread wide and fold back onto the bed, and pumped vigorously in and out of my love tunnel. The lovemaking was too overwhelming for me, and with Daryl in control, he regulated the show.

I occasionally caught eye contact with Daryl when I wasn't on my way to another climax. Daryl remained focused on my face, reading me as my head slowly rocked side to side, raising a few inches from the pillow every so often as I was overcome by his sexual techniques.

Daryl peered down at me, never losing his rhythm as he softly whispered, "Stephanie."

"Yes," I muttered back, also in a whisper.

Pumping, he continued, "You know I love you, right?"

"Oooh yes, Daryl. Oooh. I know you love me, Daryl."

He picked up his pace. "You know we'll always be together, right?"

"Oooh yes. I know, honey."

"Forever, Stephanie. Till death do us part," said Daryl, drilling like a power tool.

"Till, uhhh," I gasped, "death, oooh, do, oo, oo, us, aahhh, part, mmph."

"I'm sorry, honey, do you forgive me?" He rammed harder.

"Of course I do, honey. Oooh, oooh, oooh." I clutched Daryl's upper back and dug my fingernails deep into his skin. He knew my sexual appetite. It was easy for him to give me a clitoral climax. Bringing me over the top from a vaginal climax only happened one other time; the first time we made love. That was the only other time I dug my nails into him like I was doing just then. At the height of my orgasm, Daryl released his load and quickly ejected his battering ram from my vagina. Then he dove head first into my soaking mound. He massaged my clitoris aggressively with his fingers as his tongue danced around my swollen lips, bringing me to a double climax.

My leg shook uncontrollably. My face twisted up and I locked my thighs around my husband's head as I lifted myself at the waist almost choking him. I let out a moan so loud that even Daryl's muffled ears heard the howl.

Daryl raised one of my legs from his face and laid still for almost two minutes. As the snoring got louder, he slid from underneath my worn out ass and eased his way to the shower with a smile a mile wide sprawled across his face. Before he reached the bathroom, he turned and looked at me and quietly said, "That's my motha fuckin' pussy." He then continued on into the tub and took a long hot shower.

About an hour later, he exited the bathroom and slid back into the bed beside me. I was still sound asleep breathing like a teddy bear. *Damn, that nigga can fuck.* Daryl closed his eyes and thought, "I'm not going to cheat on her ever again." Two minutes later, he was snoring right along with me.

THE NEXT MORNING ...

I was awakened by the sound of my telephone ringing.

Ring...ring!

"Dee, ain't you gonna answer the phone?" I yelled.

Daryl was in the kitchen making some buttermilk pancakes.

Ring...ring!

"Dee...Dee!" I continued from underneath the warmth of my blanket.

"I hear it but I ain't answering it." Daryl looked over his shoulder toward the living room where he and I were shacked up all night and, with a smirk on his face, sarcastically said, "It might be one of your boyfriends." He put his hand over his mouth after he realized what he said. He couldn't risk another slip up and accusing me of something only meant that he was guilty himself.

Over the grease popping he could hear me respond, "What, nigga, I ain't you."

I finally answered the telephone and to no surprise it was my best friend Kee Kee.

"Hello," I said, removing the covers from my naked body. The sheets were tangled together and stretched across our bed.

"Bitch, you can't answer your phone?" asked Kee Kee jokingly.

"I couldn't find it," I said, shaking the hair from my face.

Daryl cleared his throat and added a little bass to his voice in case I was on the phone with a guy. Loud enough so the person on the other end of the line could hear, he yelled, "You want syrup on your pancakes?" Daryl knew I wanted syrup on my pancakes; it's the only way I'd eat them.

I immediately caught on to Daryl's game and I decided to play along.

Anxious, Kee Kee asked, "Who's there with you?"

I covered the phone and whispered into the receiver, "Daryl."

Kee Kee quickly snapped, "Bitch, I thought I told you…"

With the phone still covered, I cut Kee Kee off, "I know, I know. Just chill. We'll talk later."

"No, you didn't girl," said Kee Kee.

"Kee, he thinks you're some nigga. Just play along," I said, removing my hand from the phone.

Daryl walked over to me with a plate full of hot pancakes and a tall glass of milk. He stared at me as if he were trying to read me.

I returned the awkward glare making it so I looked suspicious.

All Daryl could hear was my side of the conversation.

"Mm hm," I mumbled. "A guy," I continued.

Daryl looked through the mirror catching a glimpse of me twirling my hair in my hand. Sitting at the end of the couch bed in his boxers, Daryl leaned back a little so he wouldn't miss anything that was being said.

"He's cool…last night…yeah, he stayed over."

Daryl couldn't take it any longer. He placed his plate on the table and turned toward me. He yelled, "Let me see that fuckin' phone, Steph!"

"For what?" I asked, griping the telephone with both hands.

"'Cause." Daryl stood up and tightened his face as if he were mad.

"Because what?"

"Because I wanna know who the fuck is that you're talking to."

I rolled my eyes and spoke into the telephone. "He wants to speak to you." I paused and twisted up my face. "I don't know...ask him...hold on."

Daryl snatched the phone from me, looked at me and gripped his crotch as a sign of authority. He clutched the telephone tightly with his other hand and spoke into the receiver like if it were a microphone and he was *LL Cool J* in that *"I'm Bad"* video. "You listen here, homie. Her husband is back, and I ain't leaving no more. So you can toss the number and don't call here again. You got that playboy? You call here one more time and I'm gonna go and get all my niggas that just came home from Attica with me and we're gonna come through there and punish something. You hear me?" Daryl didn't hear anyone respond. "Do you hear me nigga?"

"That is a damn shame," said Kee Kee.

"Nigga, put some bass..." He looked over at me but continued to talk into the receiver. "Homie, you sound like a bitch."

"Stop calling me nigga, Daryl. And I ain't no bitch neither," said Kee Kee.

"Who the...? What the...?" Looking over at me he asked, "What's this?"

"It's Kee Kee," I said, laughing with my hand out requesting the telephone. "May I have the phone back please?" I asked smiling.

He spoke into the phone. "So y'all think something is funny, huh? I knew it was your ass anyway, Kee Kee. I was just playing along with Stephanie like I ain't know. Y'all chicks can't fool me. I'm the man," said Daryl, holding his groin.

"Will you give the phone back to Stephanie already?" asked Kee Kee.

"Hold on." Daryl threw the telephone on the bed, picked up his plate of pancakes and walked back into the kitchen.

I picked up the phone and continued talking to my friend.

"You should've seen his face, Kee Kee," I said, laughing.

"I can imagine," replied Kee Kee. "Steph," said Kee Kee, sounding concerned, "you sure you know what you're doing?" Kee Kee was worried about my well being.

"I'm sure. He apologized."

Kee Kee pouted. "That nigga is always sorry...his sorry ass."

"I know, I know, Kee Kee. Look, I appreciate you always being there for me but I love him. I love Daryl so much."

"Yeah, whatever. You just got dick amnesia," she said, rolling her eyes.

Laughing, I asked, "What the hell is dick amnesia?"

"You girl. As soon as he gives you the dick, you forget about everything else," she said, laughing.

"You got that right," I laughed, then continued, "You should've seen us last night."

"Did he make it up to you?" asked Kee Kee anxiously.

"Like a motha fucka."

"Cloud nine, girl?"

"Bitch, I was on the moon." We laughed harder.

Daryl reentered the living room and noticed me having the time of my life. Seeing me like that made him think about how happy I could be and how lucky he was to have me. He kindly strolled back into the kitchen and proceeded with cleaning the dishes.

CHAPTER SEVEN

ONE MONTH LATER ...

Monica continued to call Daryl everyday. After three weeks without returning her calls, she gave up. She finally realized that he was avoiding her and gave up hope on their torrid affair. Not long after, Monica was dating a handsome heavyset guy who introduced himself as a behind the scenes music producer. Monica thought, "Whatever his occupation was, it paid well because he lived a lavish lifestyle."

Monica dated Rodney to fill the void Daryl left behind. However, she hated Rodney. The sex never lasted long enough to change positions and he was too arrogant. Monica remained in the relationship because Rodney was nice and he always treated her with the utmost respect. He also bought her extravagant gifts. On their second date, he showed up at her doorstep with a full- length blue fox fur coat. Monica was stunned, and to show her appreciation, she told him he could make love to her and that she would make it worth his while. That's when she found out that he was a one-minute man. She tried to revive him orally, but it was to no avail. She lied to Rodney, telling him that it was her first time giving someone oral sex, and when she couldn't turn his *Bruce Banner* into the *Hulk*, she forced tears from her eyes, telling him that she was embarrassed and felt like a whore. Rodney soaked it all up and promised Monica two more coats. Within the next week, she had a three-quarter length chinchilla and a white mink jacket, both with matching hats.

Daryl, on the other hand, kept to his promise. Happy that his relationship was getting back on track, he began working extra hard, bringing his workload to a minimum and ahead of schedule. He closed the deal on the company and became sole owner of 'M & M Construction.' With things on a roll, he and I decided it was time for a vacation and headed straight for the travel agency.

We booked one-way tickets for a trip to Venice, Italy. From there we headed to Paris, France.

We stayed in Venice for only a few days and did most of our cuddling near the water. We visited a historical church where we prayed among a slew of devoted Italians, and before leaving, we ended our last night with a nightcap on the monumental 'Rialto Bridge.' It was there that he promised me that he would never cause any more dissension between us again regarding another woman.

From there, Romeo and myself flew first class to Paris, France for some memorable sightseeing.

Stationed in the romantic city for only two hours, the first thing we noticed was graffiti. Someone had spray painted a picture of a character on the wall of what appeared to be a monastery or church. It was nothing like the writings we'd seen in New York City, but it certainly was worth the look.

Next, we visited the famous 'Academy of Music.' The building's architectural structure in itself was amazing. The building was huge and, upon seeing it, Daryl thought, "If I were to compare it to any structure in New York City, I would have to say it was similar to the large post office in downtown Manhattan."

Our second day in Paris, Daryl and I took a taxicab from our hotel to the world famous 'Eiffel Tower.' Approaching the marvelous fixture from the highway, one would assume the tower was narrow and probably not very tall. However, once we stopped beneath the incredible sight, the gigantic citadel reminded us of a skyscraper or fortress. Everyone was fascinated with the size of the tower. "Truly amazing!" I thought. "Truly amazing!"

Excited, myself and the Mr. didn't let up there. Like most tourists, we toured the city until we came across more famous landmarks, one of which was the 'Arc de Tramp.'

In the Soho section of New York City, you'll find a smaller replica of the 'Arc.' But in Paris, at the end of the strip called the 'Champ Elysee's,' you'll find the one and only original 'Arc.'

Resembling the front of a castle, the 'Arc' is huge with a large platform roof for tourists to view the city from different angles.

From the roof you can see the beautiful 'Eiffel Tower' and, looking in another direction, you see the famous strip called the 'Champ Elysee's.' Although this strip is known in Paris as 125th Street is known in Harlem, unlike the mecca of New York City, it has a perfume in France named after it.

The day before leaving the home of the French, Daryl and I stopped by the world famous church of 'Notre Dame.' Inside, we prayed. Daryl clutched my hand and quietly began reciting a personal supplication. He said, "Dear Lord, most gracious and most merciful. You are the one and only. The eternal. The absolute. He who begetteth not nor is He begotten. He who has none like unto Him. I seek refuge with you Lord and cherisher of mankind, from the mischief of the whisperer of evil. Please Lord, bless my wife and I with the strength to overcome our misunderstandings. Amen."

"That was beautiful," I said, standing up from my kneeled down position.

We exited the church as Daryl continued to talk. "I meant it, honey. No more whispers from the devil. It's all about us now."

We returned to our suite and cuddled under the warmth of burning logs that roasted in the hand-made fireplace in our bedroom.

BACK IN NEW YORK CITY ...

Back home, I was upstairs unpacking and separating dirty clothes for the laundry. Daryl sat by the telephone, listening to every message attentively, writing down any information that seemed vital. Just as he cleared the last message, a low beeping noise crept from a nearby drawer.

Daryl retrieved the small device and looked at its tiny screen. It read, "One Page." He pressed the button and an unfamiliar number appeared across the small lens. While I was preoccupied with the dirty laundry, Daryl snuck downstairs to retrieve his cellular phone and return the call.

He looked toward the steps that led up to our bedroom and when he felt the coast was clear, he dialed the number.

7-1-8-5-5-5-1-1-8-3

Ring…ring…ring…ring…ring!

The telephone rang five times and just as Daryl was about to hang up, someone picked up.

In a measured tone, the voice on the other end calmly said, "Hello, Daryl."

Surprised, Daryl became fidgety and almost lost his cool. His recent episode with me stuck in his head like bobby pins in a weave and he immediately regained his composure. He responded as casual as Monica did. "What, Monica?"

Impassively, she said, "All you had to do was tell me to leave you alone and I would've respected your request. It's not like I was in love with your ass or anything. It wasn't all that anyway."

Daryl chuckled. "Well, I tried to call but, you know."

Upstairs, *with my bionic ears*, I heard what sounded like conversation coming from the main floor of our home. Curious, I proceeded to investigate. I walked to the edge of the staircase and listened intently.

"So you tried to call me, Daryl?" said Monica, with an attitude that said, *"Yeah, right!"*

The house was quiet and I could hear a voice coming from the other end of the phone. It was just difficult to understand what they were saying.

"Yup."

"Yeah, whatever. Just tell me, Dee, did you really care about me?"

"Monica, listen."

I covered my mouth when I heard my husband call Monica's name. My eyes began to water and my lips started trembling.

"Did you care, Dee?" she questioned.

"Yeah, Monica, what you think, I just sleep with anybody."

I was shocked and hurt at the same time. After all we had been through, I couldn't believe my husband was on the phone in our home with the woman who caused all the drama in the first place.

"Tell me your love is strong for her and I won't bother you anymore. Tell me your love for Stephanie is real, Daryl."

"Monica," Daryl subconsciously raised his voice, "my love is real like a motha fucka."

As the words slipped from Daryl's mouth, I slid down the wall crying. My stomach felt like I just swallowed a ton of bricks. Daryl swayed backward into the sight of me staring down at him mouthing the words, "No."

When Daryl looked up, he saw me with my arms folded, clutching myself, trying to pull myself together. Daryl was speechless as he noticed the tears dripping from my eyes. Slowly his hand took on a mind of its own and in the middle of Monica's rambling, he closed his cellular phone ending the senseless call.

He called out softly. "Steph." He swallowed hard behind it.

I stared at him with a look that seemed colder than ice. I was tired of the bullshit. *I shouldn't have stayed this long.*

Daryl swallowed again, lowered his head and quietly mouthed the word, "Damn!" He looked back up at me and called out to me once again. "Steph." He noticed the tears beginning to flow more rapidly and tried once again. Unfortunately, he was unsuccessful. "Steph, please, it's not what you think. I can explain," he begged.

Before he could place one foot on the bottom step, my

heartbroken ass spoke out, "Leave!" I said firmly.

"Steph, please, I can..."

"Leave! Now!" I yelled. My eyes opened as wide as they could, stopping Daryl in his tracks. He was afraid that I would do something crazy. *"Fuck with me if you want to,"* I thought. He looked up at me with the look of a lost soul. He reached up at me and mouthed the word, "Please," one more time.

He tried to approach without me responding, but I suddenly spoke out through gritted teeth, "Daryl, if you don't leave this house right this second I will call the police and tell them you assaulted me." I was lying, but I had to say something that would make him leave.

It was nothing else he could do. He had to catch me when I was calm. And hopefully he'd be able to clear everything up. Without a second thought, Daryl turned and left the house.

CHAPTER EIGHT

THREE MONTHS LATER ...

I had had enough. One week after removing Daryl from our home, I filed for divorce. Only in the presence of my attorney was I allowed to speak with Daryl. Under the advice of my family and friends, meeting with Daryl alone would be too much for me at such a vulnerable time in my life. My lawyer, Ms. Victoria Dunn, informed me that the legal ramifications would take months before a decision would be made since tangible assets were involved. In the meantime, the Honorable Ruth McLymont, the presiding judge in the case, granted me temporary ownership of our Mt. Vernon home. However, Daryl was allowed to keep his truck because his attorney, Mr. Michael F. Cappellano, emphasized the fact that Daryl had to travel to and from work and I didn't.

Thirty-five days after our separation, I found out I was six weeks pregnant. *What a fucked up time to have a bun in the oven.* Daryl was notified but reminded that he must stay away from me until the divorce was final. In the meantime, he continued running his company with the help of his friend, Tommy, while I went back to work at the bank.

I was eager to return back to the Chase Bank of America, located on 131st Street and 34th Avenue, in the South Jamaica section of Queens. My old boss, Mr. Frederick Morse, welcomed me back with open arms, and because I made employee of the month almost every month that I was employed there, he made an effort to give me back my position as bank manager. My job description was to handle all large transactions, make sure all of the drawers were kept full and to monitor all monetary withdrawals and deposits at the drive-thru's automated teller machine.

Nine weeks back at my old spot and I was performing as if I had never left. Cruising behind the bank's counter like a supermodel strolls down a runway, I made my way to window #4 to accommodate a fellow coworker. Amy Boucher, a 19-year-old Albanian girl with long blonde hair, dark green eyes and a large nose needed my assistance.

Arriving at the window, I slid up beside Amy and kindly asked, "Amy, your help light is illuminated. Do you need any assistance?" I glanced at the customer, an almond-complexioned man with brown chestnut eyes and long eyelashes, returned my gaze back to Amy and continued, "May I help you with anything?"

"Yes, Mrs. Manning," replied Amy in her schoolgirl drawl. Shyly, she looked at me without making direct eye contact and said, "This customer has a cashier's check for eighty thousand dollars. What do I do?"

I motioned with my hand for Amy to scoot over and with the confidence of a leader, I benignly asked the guy, "May I see the check, please?"

The customer slid the check under the small transparent partition, allowing his hand to gently touch mine and when I looked up at him, he smiled flirtingly. Catching me off guard, I returned the smile and said, "One moment sir. I'll be right back." I turned and walked toward the rear of the bank.

The customer, Mr. Roger Lowe, property owner of Green Acres Mall, Sunrise Movie Theater and the luxury homes of Jamaica Estates, all properties in Queens, glanced over at Amy who waited nervously for her superior, me, to verify the transaction.

I returned to the window, caught eye contact with Roger and with a smile faker than a four dollar bill, cordially said, "Mr. Lowe, sorry for the inconvenience. How would you like your bills, sir?"

Roger returned the smile and simply replied, "One hundred dollar bills please. Thank you ma'am." He nodded and caught a quick glimpse of the area of my finger where my wedding ring used to be. A quick thought entered Roger's mind and before I could walk away, he asked, "Excuse me, Ms..." he paused, looked at my nametag and continued, "...Ms. Manning, I brought along my briefcase that I use to carry large amounts of cash. Would it be a problem if I accompany you and have the money placed in my case?"

"Of course not, Mr. Lowe. Come along. Right this way please." I motioned with a wave of my hand for Roger to follow me.

Roger trailed me to a nearby cubicle where the money was counted, wrapped and placed neatly into his briefcase. As the process went underway, Roger made small conversation.

Clearing his throat, he pleasantly asked, "So, are you married?"

I never took my eyes off the money machine as I counted and recounted each ten thousand dollar stack of one hundred dollar bills. I shot back without missing a beat. "Used to be."

"Used to be?" he asked. Then added, "But not anymore?"

"Not anymore," I responded, still focusing on the money counter.

"How long's it been?" he asked.

"How long's what been?" I asked, bringing my eyes to his as I wrapped the second stack of bills neatly next to the first stack. I then reached for the next batch of bills and began counting them up.

Roger chuckled because a crazy thought came across his mind. He guessed I was referring to sex when I asked him to what he was referring when he asked me, "How long's it been?"

I looked at him and smiled. "What's so funny, Mr. Lowe?"

Laughing softly, Roger said, "Nothing. Just a thought."

I knew he was flirting. It had been years since I felt free enough to return the friendly gesture so I took it upon myself to express my liberty. Stopping in mid count, I asked, "Care to share your thoughts?"

"How about over some dinner?" he asked.

"Sorry," I said with a smile. I continued to count the money. Roger wouldn't let up. "Why not?" he asked.

"Because it hasn't been long."

Confused, Roger asked, "What hasn't been long? The last time you ate?"

"No silly. You asked me how long it's been." I paused for a second to get my words together. Then I said, "It hasn't been long since we separated." I slid Roger a third stack and began on the fourth.

The two of us sat silently as I finished up counting Roger's money. Contemplating his next approach, Roger waited until I packed the last stack into his briefcase. I closed it, locked it and proceeded to stand up. I slid the valise filled with money across the tiny table and held my hand out to him.

"Thanks for doing business with us, Mr. Lowe. Please come again."

Roger took my hand into his, brought it close to his mouth and kissed it. He looked into my eyes and said, "I will, Ms. Manning. Trust me, I will." *He was fine as hell too.*

He released my hand, grabbed his belongings and headed for the door. Feeling my eyes burning into his back, Roger strolled out of the bank as cool as he could ever be.

I smiled to myself and thought, "Oh, I miss Daryl so much." I rubbed my stomach as an affectionate gesture to my unborn child and continued to ponder. "I wonder how life is going to be for my child without the full time presence of its father." I sighed. "Oh Lord, please give me strength."

In the days that followed, flowers, cards and candy poured in from couriers of various businesses. Each gift arrived with a complimentary card. When the first bouquet of yellow friendship roses arrived, the accompanying written message read,

"Roses are red, but yours are not,

Yellow's for friendship, just open your heart..."

The following day, a box of chocolate-covered strawberries arrived in a basket filled with other chocolate treats. The card that accompanied the candy also had a sweet message. It read,

"Your name should be Sugah, because you're sweet,

Just make it one date, and make it my treat…"

When a second set of flowers arrived on the third day, this time with pink rose petals, I was overwhelmed by the expression and became emotional when I read the note. It said,

"Ms. Manning, you are the most beautiful woman I have ever laid my eyes on. I sent the pink roses because I think I'm getting warm. When the red ones arrive, that'll mean I've found what I've been searching for all my life. Stop me whenever or allow me to continue. My number is on the back. I'll be waiting."

It was signed, "Sincerely, Roger." I subconsciously placed my hand over my mouth as I read the heartfelt message. I turned the card over to its backside to examine the number and was kindly interrupted by a fellow coworker.

Standing only a few feet away, Amy Boucher swayed bashfully side to side as she called out my name. With her hands clasped behind her back, Amy quietly called out, "Mrs. Manning."

At first I didn't respond. I was too caught up in the moment. It wasn't until I felt Amy's little hand touching my arm that I acknowledged her. She called out to me again, "Mrs. Manning."

Smiling, I turned to Amy and said, "Yes, Amy."

"I'm sorry if I interrupted anything, Mrs. Manning, but someone is at your cubicle waiting for you." She pointed in the direction of my work area.

Tapping Amy's arm softly, I said, "No, you didn't interrupt anything." Looking at my cubicle, I noticed a pair of men's shoes and immediately became excited. Looking at Amy I smiled and said, "Thank you. I'm on my way."

I strolled over to my cubicle, pulling on my clothes and fixing my hair in an attempt to straighten anything out that wasn't proportioned right, and when I got to my cube, my heart dropped when I spotted Daryl fiddling with the roses that sat on top of my desk. I peered down at him and calmly asked, "Excuse me, are you supposed to be here?"

Daryl was dressed in a beige linen Armani suit with navy blue ostrich skin shoes to match his navy blue silk shirt. He looked up at me, brought his eyes back to the pink roses and said, "I was just about to ask myself the same thing."

I folded my arms, lowered my voice and said, "Daryl, you know we were advised to stay away from one another."

Lowering his voice as well he said, "I know, Steph. I just want to open an account."

"An account for what?" I whispered, as I walked around to the front of my desk. I took a seat and pulled myself close to my computer.

Daryl bit his top lip to prevent himself from smiling. He sensed that I noticed it and lowered his head to speak. "It's for my son."

"Your son!" I shouted. I was surprised. *For a minute I thought the nigga had another child by someone else.*

"Or my daughter," he said, putting his finger over his lip signaling me to lower my tone. "Whatever it is you're carrying, I'd like to open up an account or get some CDs or something so when you move on," he said, looking over at the flowers and sliding the basket of candy over, "our child will be okay and not need the assistance of some other person."

"Daryl, I'm not thinking about nobody else right now or moving on. The person who sent me these flowers and candy means nothing to me. He's just a customer pleased with our service. I'm pregnant and all that's important to me right now is the welfare of our child. To make sure our baby is healthy. Now, if you would really like to open up an account for our child, let me give you some brochures to read explaining the different accounts that are optional for unborns and toddlers."

He smiled, "I miss you, Stephanie. And whether you believe me or not, that day, I was not talking to Monica as a lover or whatever. We were not dealing with one another then. I did admit to the affair, but that last time, it was already over. I was just clarifying it with her."

"Well let me clarify something with you, Mister. You hurt me Daryl and I really think you should leave. Please," I said, as my eyes watered. I leaned back and stared at him as I tapped one of my feet.

"Do you like him, Steph?" he asked, looking into my eyes.

I moved my hand from my mouth, looked at Daryl and asked, "Like who?"

He touched the flowers again and said, "Him."

"Daryl, I told you I don't even know him like that."

He stared at me with his puppy dog eyes. "Do you still love me, Steph, because I still love you?"

"Daryl, I will always love you. But right now I'm not feeling you. I'm still hurting and I really think that you should go." The tears were forming again.

Daryl touched my hand and said, "I'm sorry, I didn't mean to get you all worked up. But remember, whenever you're ready to stop working and relax, only for the baby," he said, rising from his seat, "let me know and I will become your number one provider. I promise I will be at your every beck and call, day and night, Stephanie." He gave me one long emotional stare, then headed out.

I watched him drive off and plopped down into my chair. I leaned my head back, looked up at the ceiling fans that spun slowly and sighed. I thought for a second, then got up and grabbed the flowers and candy off of my desk. Again I sighed. I then proceeded to drop everything into my trashcan. I looked over at the line of tellers and noticed three of them had their help lights illuminated. I made my way toward the nearest teller and silently thought to myself, "What am I doing? I must put an end to Roger's advances and focus more on my priorities, my child. And I have to learn how to love Daryl from a distance as well."

Later on that evening I called Roger and explained to him that I wasn't ready to deal with anybody at the moment. I told him that perhaps one day he and I may meet up again, and if fate has its way, then more power to us. Until then, I'd rather deal with my issues as a single woman. I told Roger how I felt and he kindly respected my wishes.

CHAPTER NINE

At his new home, alone one evening with nothing to do, Daryl clicked on his computer and began browsing the Internet. Having spent the past twenty minutes watching the news, Daryl realized he had some free time on his hands. Instead of staying glued to the idiot box, Daryl decided to log online and riffle through various websites, one of which caught his attention. Dateme.com was a website many of his coworkers talked about at work. They expressed to one another how much their lives had changed romantically because of the website.

He entered the domain full of curiosity and ended up in a chat room full of available bachelors and bachelorettes. Narrowing his selection to *'singles'*, Daryl was taken aback by how accessible single women were, as well as the large number of eligible ladies that were out there searching for a partner and were now at the push of a button. Fed up, he thought for a moment, "If Stephanie won't be with me, someone else will."

Daryl pressed the "enter" button on his keypad and anxiously waited for his next set of online instructions. The screen blinked and when it settled, a description list appeared, allowing Daryl the option to choose to his liking. Daryl rolled the mouse, moving the cursor to a selection box that read *'singles'*, and clicked the button. Another long list appeared and Daryl clicked everywhere he felt necessary. At the selection box marked, *'preference'*, he paused and quietly spoke to himself. "Preference really isn't an issue with me as long as the woman is a decent lady." Before he pressed the button on the mouse, he made a mental analyzation. "I really need someone that has the same understandings that I have and one who can identify with my struggle. Then again, white women seem to be able to understand my black brothers today more so than ever. Plus, they know their place in the relationship." Daryl moved the cursor back over to the *'preference'* area and clicked on the box that read *'SWF'* for single white female.

He continued clicking various description boxes distinguishing women by their size, shape, age and education. Daryl was impressed learning that so many Caucasian women had their lives set when it came to their careers and family values. He just couldn't understand why so many of them were single and had no one to share it with.

He finally entered some information stating that he wanted to hear from a white woman between twenty-one and thirty-five years of age, 150 pounds or under and no children.

After typing in his interests, Daryl pressed "enter." The screen went blue and the words *'please wait'* appeared in a box that flashed off and on. After a few minutes, the screen returned to its blank page and the words "Hi, my name is Susan Blanchett. What's yours?" appeared soon afterward.

Surprised, Daryl quickly typed in his own name and decided to add a little touch to his response. He typed in, "Hello, my name is Daryl. How do you do?" He leaned back and placed his hands behind his head as a response quickly appeared on his computer. And just as quickly as Susan would type things in, Daryl was right there to respond, forming an online relationship with Ms. Susan Blanchette.

"I'm fine," Susan typed. "Do you mind describing yourself to me?" she asked.

Daryl leaned in and punched in the words, "I'm 6'2", 200 pounds. I work out four times a week and I barely have any fat on my frame. I'm outgoing and very athletic. I'm a chocolate-skinned African American heterosexual with no health problems and I own my own business. I'll be twenty-five years old in a few short months and I am very much single." Daryl thought about pressing the "enter" button, but before he ended his message, he entered, "How about you? Tell me a little bit about yourself." Daryl pressed "enter" and patiently waited for a response. After a grueling two minutes, a photo selection of Ms. Susan Blanchette with a short bio appeared on the screen. Daryl was floored by her response. He said to himself as he looked at the photos, "Damn, white people are somewhat different from black people. For one," he said, tapping his chin with his right index finger, "they be prepared like a motha."

Susan made four photos available for anyone interested. She also listed her age, occupation and hobbies. All of her pictures were professionally done by a studio photographer and they were all photos of her in bikini bathing suits. If Susan wouldn't have listed that one of her great grandparents was Italian, Daryl would've sworn she had African American blood in her from the way her physique was built. Susan had firm, double C cup breasts, a small waist and wide hips. Her butt wasn't as plump as Daryl had wished, but for a white woman, "baby had back." She was a twenty-seven-year-old brunette with long shiny hair that fell halfway down her back and her tan was flawless. She had blue eyes and a small mole above her top lip that reminded Daryl of Marilyn Monroe. He rated her on a scale of one to ten and gave her an eight. That was sufficient enough for him.

For the next couple of hours the duo traded information, learning everything they could about one another. Daryl learned that Susan also worked out. And instead of the usual hobbies like camping, fishing, hiking and horseback riding, which Susan thought were boring, he learned that she was an outdoor adventurous person that loved challenges, which is why she was an amateur race car driver and a dance choreographer. She also loved playing Monopoly, which was one of his favorite games as well.

Daryl experienced a sense of well being chatting with Susan and his feelings compelled him to ask her out on a date. She agreed and, at 7 p.m. that evening, the couple met up at a bar and grill in upper Manhattan.

Daryl thought he would feel uncomfortable hanging out with a white woman, especially with all the talk about, "As soon as a black man gets himself established financially, he gives himself to a white woman," but the entire time they spent out that evening seemed normal to the both of them. They felt so comfortable laughing and sharing stories together that when the night seemed to be turning into morning, Daryl had no problem asking Susan back to his place.

Just finishing a chuckle from a hilarious story that Susan shared with him, Daryl looked at his watch and calmly said, "Wow, it's getting late, Suzie." Over the course of the evening,

Susan and Daryl agreed that blacks and whites have names so similar but yet so different since black people put a twist on anything that they can call their own. So the two, as a sign of mutual understanding, decided that Susan's special name for Daryl would be Suzie and Daryl would remain Daryl because Dee reminded him too much of his wife. Anyway, Daryl continued to chat with his date, "Are you ready to leave?" he asked.

Susan was a little tipsy. They both were. However, they made sure both of them were sober enough to drive home in case something happened with one of their vehicles. The city was in a deficit and towing people's cars in unauthorized areas seemed to be a sure way to help out with the debt.

Smiling, Susan rolled her eyes seductively at Daryl and said, "I almost fell asleep waiting for you to ask me back to your place." They both laughed.

Daryl asked, "Do you want me to drive you and you park your car?"

Susan removed herself from his warm embrace, caressed his bald head flirtingly while staring into his eyes and said, "I'm a big girl, Daryl. I'll need to get myself home in the morning anyway." Then she spun around and walked toward the parking lot where their vehicles were parked.

At Daryl's apartment, the two lust birds found their way into Daryl's living room and sat comfortably together on his sofa. Susan slithered close to Daryl on the couch and began nibbling on his ear. Smelling her perfume and feeling her breasts brush up against his arm, Daryl started to get a rise in his pants and Susan noticed it.

Susan stared at Daryl's crotch as she continued whispering sweet nothings into his ear. She moved even closer to him, licking her lips and panting. Suddenly, she reached out and wrapped her hand around his protruding member.

"Oh, my God!" she gasped at the size of his penis. "You're immense!" she bellowed quietly.

Daryl chuckled and thought to himself, "I guess it's true what they say about black men and the size of our third leg."

She unzipped his fly and pulled out his love stick. "Wow, you're so hard. So big and hard," said Susan, leaning over. She began showering his schwanz with passionate kisses. Her long, sexy fingernails were digging deep into Daryl's thighs as she swallowed his sausage inch by inch until as much as she could possibly hold was in her mouth.

Releasing her suction, she looked up and said, "I need a fucking." She groaned, pressed her breasts against Daryl's chest and said, "Give me what I need. Please fuck me. Please, please!" She grabbed Daryl aggressively by his shirt collar.

Daryl didn't need to be begged. He was suffering from losing his wife and vulnerable to anyone who provoked him. "Damn, Suzie, you're a horny little mama, aren't you?" he asked, looking her in her eyes. He pulled out a condom and put it on.

Suzie replied by raising her skirt revealing a pantyless shaved mound. She leaned back on the sofa, grabbed her ankles and pulled her legs apart. Daryl lunged forward and buried his cock into her tiny pink hole. He then began a piston-like motion that drove Susan crazy. He rammed her for close to forty minutes and when she couldn't take it anymore, she whispered into his ear, "Come for me."

Eager to oblige, Daryl clutched both ends of the back pillow that supported Suzie and pumped in and out of her like a madman. He didn't realize his own strength. He was pushing

Susan up the pillow with each of his manly thrustings. He kept his eyes closed until he exploded everything he had into the condom. Afterward, the duo collapsed in a sweaty pile.

Daryl kept his member lodged in Susan's tunnel until his meatstick went limp. "Are you okay in there, baby?" she asked. She patted him on his back lightly and said, "Don't worry about me, I'll be okay. Take all the time you need."

Daryl rolled off of Susan and walked into the bathroom. He let his trousers drop to the floor and pulled the condom off his penis. He dropped it into the toilet and flushed it down the drain. Daryl turned, looked into the mirror and began examining his face. Wiping the sweat from his brow, he mumbled, "Damn, what the fuck am I doing?" He turned on the water, grabbed a washcloth from a nearby shelf and wiped his member clean. He then fixed his clothes and walked back into his living room.

Susan stood up fully clothed and nervously said, "I can leave now if you want me to."

"You know what, Suzie, sit down." He motioned for her to take a seat next to him and gently grabbed her hand. He began caressing it as he calmly spoke. "Susan, you're a terrific person." She lowered her gaze foreseeing what was about to come next. Daryl raised her head by grabbing her by her chin and said, "Look at me, Suz, I can't do this," he sighed. "I still love my wife and I just realized it. I can't go into another relationship with any baggage because it wouldn't be healthy. For any of us. I really don't know what to say except to perhaps give it some time. If it works itself out, I'll give you my all, but until I'm sure, I don't think we should see one another anymore. I'm sorry, Susan, I really am," he said, shaking his head.

Susan put her finger up to Daryl's lips indicating that he didn't need to say anything else. She got the picture. She moved closer to him and gazed into his chestnut eyes. She gave him a peck on his forehead and said, "Listen, I know. I know how it is. I've been there before myself. Now tonight was great and I really enjoyed myself. You're a very sweet guy. Gorgeous too! And a great lover, but there's more to you than just that. And if I can't have all of you now, call me when I can. I'll be waiting."

Just then, they both stood up. Susan kissed Daryl on the lips and walked out of his apartment. Daryl stood there in a trance, traumatized by the idea that his wife may no longer be in love with his ass.

CHAPTER TEN

At five months pregnant, I still maintained my sexiness. Though my face filled out, my skin remained clear and my hair had grown a full two-and-a-half inches. I put on twelve pounds and the weight went straight to my chest and backside, giving me a more voluptuous look. At work, my coworkers playfully teased me about my new walk. I wobbled and it reminded them of the ducks that roamed the neighborhood pond.

Occasionally, Daryl would stop by and drop off bag lunches to me, usually consisting of tuna fish sandwiches and pickles. To keep my stress at a minimum, he would never press me about our relationship. As far as he knew, the divorce was still in progress and the chances of reconciling our relationship were slim.

As I sashayed my pregnant self from one teller to the next checking for any problems and assisting anyone who needed help, a customer entered my worksite and was about to turn my ordinary day into mayhem.

Approaching teller number two, the customer reached into her purse and retrieved her identification card. She said to the teller, "Excuse me, I'm having trouble with my credit card. May I speak with your manager please?" She continued searching her bag for the card.

"One moment please." Amy pressed the help button attached to her drawer and her "assistance sign" instantly illuminated. I noticed the call for help and confidently strolled over to Amy's window.

I introduced myself as the bank's manager and inquired about the problem. "Good afternoon, ma'am. My name is Stephanie Manning and I am the bank's manager. May I be of any assistance to you?"

Too busy rumbling through her handbag, the customer never caught my name. All she heard was, "May I be of any assistance to you?"

Sliding her I.D. and credit card toward me, she spoke out, "Yes, my name is Monica Hartridge and I'm having a problem with my credit card. Everytime..."

My mind went blank after I realized who was standing right in front of me. I could've recognized the voice a mile away. The woman I accused of being a home wrecker finally met face to face with me. I placed my hands over my mouth and began to shake lightly.

Monica and Amy noticed what was happening and Amy immediately responded. "Mrs. Manning, Mrs. Manning," she said nervously. "Is it the baby?"

"Oh my God," whispered Monica. "I hope this lady isn't going into labor."

Amy rushed to retrieve a chair and a glass of water for me but, with the wave of a hand, I declined.

I regained my composure and said, "Ms. Hartridge, my name is Stephanie Manning. Will you follow me over to my office?"

"Are you sure you're okay, Mrs. Manning?" asked Amy, concerned with my supervisor's condition.

"I'll manage," I said, never taking my eyes off of Monica. We entered my office like two the hard way with me closing the door behind Monica. Amy watched as I closed the blinds. She figured everything was okay from there. Just as she went to dim her light, in walked *stupid ass* himself.

"Excuse me, Ms. Boucher, is Stephanie in today?" asked Daryl cordially.

"Yes, she's here. She's talking to a customer in her office, but I don't think she wants to be bothered right now," said Amy.

Daryl felt his stomach tighten up. As confident as he was, he dreaded the day that he would have to confront the man that was sending me flowers and candy. With a hint of jealousy, he asked, "Is she in with a male or female?"

Amy knew about the whole marriage and divorce situation that we were experiencing. After working a few months at my beck and call, myself and the eager subordinate became close associates and talked about everything from school to careers and men. Amy heard about the affair Daryl had but the name of the woman he cheated with was never an issue. Neither Daryl nor Amy knew that the woman who contributed to the downfall of my relationship sat only a few yards away.

Curious, Daryl walked over to my office and tapped lightly on the door. He could hear commotion coming from inside but the heavy duty steel door muffled most of the sound. My voice got louder as I neared the door and, without peering out to see who it was that was knocking, my upset mom-to-be ass swung the door open and angrily said, "What do you want?"

I immediately caught eye contact with Daryl and, as quickly

as our two eyes met, I turned my head toward Monica who was standing at the opposite side of my desk. Daryl peered inside to see who I was talking to and as soon as he noticed it was Monica, his jaw dropped. He suddenly took on a look that said, "What the fuck!"

We both stared at Daryl diligently as he stood in awe at the surprise meeting. I stood in the doorway with my arms crossed, leaning most of my weight to my right side and tapped my left foot. Monica stood silently with her hand on her hip, chewing on a piece of bubblegum and rolling her eyes at her former plaything. *Her ass was too shook to look at me.*

"Did I interrupt anything?" he asked nervously. He brought his gaze back and forth to both of us while simultaneously forcing a fake smile.

"I think you need to come in here and have a seat, playboy," I said. Monica stopped chewing, looked at me, while I was still staring at Daryl, then blew a bubble.

Amy watched everything unfold. When I closed the door behind Daryl, Amy flinched when it slammed. When Amy was ten years old, doctors determined she was suffering from paranoia. Her mother rushed her to a doctor one day when she was younger because she suspected her daughter was being tormented by someone or something. However, through numerous tests, it was determined that she inherited the condition from the sudden change of environments. She lived in the eastern European country of Albania from birth until she was almost ten years old. Her mom suddenly moved their entire family, at the request of Amy's father, who was already in America, to the United States. It was then that her abnormal behavior began. When the entrance bell sounded, Amy looked over toward the front of the bank and didn't notice anything unusual. In fact, the person who just entered the bank was a friend of mine.

Amy waved, grabbing the attention of my friend who decided to walk over to her and find out what the young lady was so excited about.

Approaching the window, the lady kindly asked, "Hey, Amy, is your boss in today?" She leaned on the counter.

"Yes, she is," replied Amy. Amy shrugged her shoulders and said, "Kee Kee, I think Mrs. Manning is having a bad day today. She seems pretty upset."

While resting one of her arms on the counter, raising her eyebrows and looking in the direction of my office, Kee Kee hesitantly asked, "What's going on? Why would you say that?"

"Because," whispered Amy, "some lady walked in here a few minutes ago claiming her credit card wasn't working and…"

Kee Kee cut her off. "So?"

"Weeell, something this woman said must've startled Mrs. Manning because after hearing whatever the statement or message was, Mrs. Manning started to shake as if she were about to have the baby or a nervous breakdown or something."

"What?" said Kee Kee, walking toward my office.

"But wait," yelled Amy, walking beside her from behind the counter. "There's more."

Kee Kee stopped, turned around and walked back over to Amy. "There's more?" asked Kee Kee. She looked back over at my office door as she patiently waited for an explanation.

"Yes." Amy took a deep breath and continued. "So I ran to get Mrs. Manning a chair and a glass of water to calm her down or whatever and, out of nowhere, she pulls herself together and did like this," said Amy, demonstrating with her hand how

I waved her away. "Then she introduced herself to the woman and requested that the lady follow her to her office."

"So what's the big deal, Amy?" Kee Kee was getting agitated because she felt that I may need her assistance and Ms. Boucher was giving her the run around.

"A few minutes after they both went into the office, Daryl walked in," said Amy, biting on her fingernail.

"Which Daryl? Her ex?" asked Kee Kee, with doubt in her voice.

"Um hmm," said Amy nodding her head aggressively.

"That no good motha...where's he at?"

"He walked over to Mrs. Manning's office and knocked. And when Mrs. Manning opened the door, she gave him a mean look that said, "Come and get your trash," said Amy, illustrating her story with funny faces, a shimmy of her neck and a few hand movements.

"Is that right?" said Kee Kee, turning towards the office once again. "I'll handle it from here, Amy. Thank you." Kee Kee proceeded towards my private work quarters and banged on the door.

Boom! Boom! Boom!

Amy nervously paced back and forth, occasionally glancing over at Kee Kee, as my best friend waited for a response.

Daryl opened the door at my request and everyone became quiet as Kee Kee stood in the doorway like Superman coming to save the day.

Kee Kee looked Daryl up and down and rolled her eyes. She looked at me and I gave two quick nods toward Monica. Kee Kee glanced at Monica, looked back over at Daryl, who was standing like a dumbfounded little child and asked, "What's going on, Steph?"

"Daryl and his girlfriend here," I said with a nod, "decided to pay me a visit today."

"Bitch, I told you he's not my man. You can have his sorry ass," said Monica. Forcing her words over Daryl's because he was responding to my comment as well.

"That ain't my girl, Kee Kee, damn! Listen." He paused. "Aye, you listening, Monica? I mean Steph? I mean Kee Kee?" Daryl was looking at Kee Kee as if she were Roy Jones, Jr. and about to knock his head off.

"No, he didn't call me that bitch's name," said Kee Kee, wiggling her neck like a snake and rolling here eyes.

"Bitch?" yelled Monica.

"Yes, he did," I said smiling. Daryl knew just as well as I did that Kee Kee was ignorant and would start trouble just about anywhere.

"Chill out y'all," said Daryl.

"No, fuck that! This bitch called me a bitch and I'm not having it," said Monica, removing her earrings.

"Oh, you wanna get crazy, bitch?" Kee Kee also began taking off her earrings and removing her high heeled shoes.

Daryl crept in between the two ladies while I slid around the desk behind Monica. "Whup her ass, Kee! Whup that bitch's ass!" I yelled.

Monica got nervous and tried to exit the office by creeping around Daryl. Kee Kee reached over Daryl and grabbed Monica by her hair which caused Monica to start swinging and scratching. I started moving furniture, hoping to prevent anything from breaking, and when Amy heard the noise from the chairs and desk sliding around, she rushed to my aid. Amy pushed the door open, striking Daryl and Monica.

Amy got scared, covered her mouth and quietly mouthed, "I'm sorry." Then she yelled out to security. "Perkins! Perkins! They're fighting in here!" she said, pointing toward my office.

Perkins, a white man, 6'4", 200 pounds and a war veteran, also ran to my aid.

After about thirty minutes, Amy was back at her window helping customers. Perkins had returned to his post near the entrance, Daryl and Monica, who were both ejected from the bank, were on their separate ways, minding their own business and Kee Kee and I conversed over cups of coffee at a nearby restaurant.

"You should've seen Daryl's face," said Kee Kee, laughing.

"I did. He was scared at shit," I said, sipping on my cappuccino.

"Ooooh girl! I wanted to beat that bitch's ass, with her little fat self," said Kee Kee, matter-of-factly.

I rolled my eyes before sipping again and said, "Had I not been pregnant, I would've handled it."

"Did they come up there together?" Kee Kee asked.

"No, I made that part up. Daryl has been coming around a lot since I've been poking out. Trying to make up and shit."

"I know you ain't falling for his bullshit again, Steph." She looked at me like I was crazy.

"Hell no!" I said.

"Her sandals were ugly as hell, too. I wonder what Daryl saw in her high yellow ass. With her big ol' butt." She sucked her teeth.

"You said it, Kee. That big ol' butt," we both said at the same time, laughing.

"I have to admit, she was pretty though," I said.

"What, Steph? I know you ain't taking sides with that whore." Kee Kee gave me a look that said she was disgusted.

"What, I ain't saying I'm cool with the bitch or anything like that. I'm just saying my man has a little taste, that's all," I said, smirking.

"I guess if I hadn't shown up, you three would've been all lovey dovey in that office of yours."

"Shut up, Kee." I was laughing again. "Don't hate 'cause I ain't experimental like you."

"Steph, ain't nothing wrong with a little tongue every now and then. I'm not a lesbian. I just don't want a dick poking me all the damn time." Closing her eyes and imagining a woman between her thighs, Kee Kee continued as she caressed herself. "There's nothing like a soft, warm, moist tongue that knows what to do and where to lick." Kee Kee opened her eyes to emphasize the latter part of her statement. She closed them again and returned to her erotic speech. "To just massage you and taste you and suck up all of your delicious juices, uuug-ghhh!" she gasped.

Kee Kee was all caught up in the moment when a gay waiter walked over to our table, rolled his eyes while snapping his fingers and asked, "Anything else, Miss Dramatic?"

Kee Kee snapped out of her performance. She glanced at me while I was laughing my ass off, looked back over at the waiter and said, "Just a small glass of ice, Miss. I think I need to cool myself off."

The waiter walked off and mumbled, "I bet you do. Women, uugh! They all wish they could be me."

Kee Kee looked at me and asked, "Was his ass gay, or just

feminine like a motha fucka?"

"Shiiit, ain't that much feminism at a women's day parade. Homeboy was gay as all outdoors."

The two of us laughed and laughed as we cleansed our minds of all the drama that was happening in and around our lives.

CHAPTER ELEVEN

E ighteen months later, Daryl and I were officially divorced. I was awarded our Mt. Vernon home, monthly alimony, child support payments, and partial custody of our fourteen-month-old daughter, Daphne.

Daryl was allowed to keep his Land Rover truck and remain at his Co-Op City apartment. He was also awarded weekends, holidays and the summer season to be able to spend quality time with his daughter.

Both of us moved on and, during the months we were separated, we each encountered different experiences with other people.

The day Daryl signed his annulment papers, he met a Puerto Rican girl named Marisol. Little did he know that a little baby daddy drama could turn out to be one crazy situation.

Driving his 4x4 past Yankee Stadium, he spotted the Spanish sexpot relaxing on a bench sucking on a lollipop. Assuming the young lady was alone, Daryl pulled his SUV around the corner and into a parking space. He jumped out, pressed a button on his key chain, triggering his alarm system, bent the corner, walked over to the bench and sat down beside the Latin love doll.

Marisol turned to look at Daryl and when he gazed back, she seductively sucked the blow pop into her mouth, gave it a twist with her thumb and forefinger, pulled it back out, looked at it, then inserted it back into her mouth again.

Daryl watched her closely and when she made the sucker disappear for a third time, he laughed, causing his shoulders to rattle with each giggle. Smiling, she pulled the candy from her kisser, smacked the roof of her mouth with her tongue giving it a light popping sound and said to the handsome young man beside her, "What you laughing at, Papa?" She brought her eyes to his and waited for Daryl to answer.

Daryl raised his head, returned Marisol's stare and replied, "You. That trick you just did with the lollipop was amazing."

Marisol sucked again and said, "I'm not doing any tricks. The tricks are what got me them." She turned her head in the direction of three young Spanish boys playing catch with a softball in the park behind them. She continued, "This is just practice." Then she smiled.

Daryl felt his penis tingle and quietly mumbled to himself, "Damn!"

When Marisol realized that Daryl was undressing her with his imagination, she broke his momentary coma by reaching her hand out to him and introducing herself. She said, "Hi, my name is Marisol. What's yours?" She rolled the letter 'R' in her name, using her Latin dialect, which turned Daryl on even more.

"My name is Daryl," he replied and shook her hand.

"You from this neighborhood, no?" asked Marisol.

"Nah, not really. I'm from Brooklyn, but I live in the Bronx."

She took another lick of her lollipop, kicked her short legs that hung from the bench and innocently asked, "Donde?"

"Donde?" asked Daryl, confused.

"Where? Where at in the Bronx joo live?" she asked, with her Spanish accent in full swing.

"I live in Co-Op."

"Co-Op City?" she asked.

"Yeah."

"What section? I got family up there."

"Section five," Daryl lied. Never was he going to expose his exact whereabouts to a perfect stranger, even if she was pretty and had a nice body.

"My family is from section one," said Marisol.

"Is that where you live?" he asked.

She shook her head, "Uh uh." She took the rest of the blow pop into her mouth, bit it away from its stick and chewed it into the form of bubble gum. Then she said, "I live here, around the corner on Jerome Avenue," she said, pointing.

"Are those your sons?" asked Daryl, nodding in the direction of the three young boys playing catch.

"Yup. My little Diablos," said Marisol, referring to her sons as little devils. "That's Juan about to throw the ball, he's five," she said, pointing at one of her children. "His brother, Raoul, who just caught it, he's six, and that's Juan who's just now catching, he's seven."

"Nah," said Daryl, confused, "you just said the little one with the blue baseball cap was Juan, right?"

"Si, yes. I got two Juan's," she said, matter-of-factly. Marisol saw the bewildered look on Daryl's face and figured she should explain. "La grande Juan, the big one, his father's name is Juan, and Popito, little Juan, his father, cabrones, is also named Juan," she said, cursing the youngest boy's father.

"Different dads?" asked Daryl.

"Yup," said Marisol, nodding her head.

"And what about Raoul?"

"His papi's name is Big Raoul."

"Three baby daddies?" asked Daryl, frowning up his face. Marisol started laughing. "Si, three holes in my ass," said Marisol, rolling her 'R' again in the word 'three' as well as saying her phrases in her best mixed up English.

Daryl tried hard not to laugh.

"What?" asked Marisol. "What about you? Any little ones?" she asked lowering her gaze to see Daryl's bent over facial expression.

As Daryl was about to answer, a small two-door Toyota Corolla pulled up with Salsa music blaring from its speakers. A Spanish guy wearing a pair of dark sunglasses was hanging halfway out of the passenger side window as the tiny Japanese vehicle came to a halt.

The driver lowered the volume so that his friend could speak. "Marisol, joo fucking got Juan out here looking like a piece of chit," yelled the guy with a heavy Latin dialect.

Marisol stood up and interjected, "Listen maricón," she cursed him, "that's my son. I feed him, I clothe him, I dress him, I wash his ass, you don't do chit," she said, pointing her finger at her chest.

"Cállate! Cállate, coño!" said Juan senior, telling Marisol to shut up using profanity for emphasis. He exited the car and brought his face close to hers. "That's me hijo too and I tell you how to dress him!" he said firmly.

Shimmying her neck, causing her long ponytail to swing

side to side, she shot back, "Fuck you, maricón. You ain't shit!"

"Puta, you ain't shit," replied Juan.

At that point, Daryl decided to walk off. He figured Marisol had too much drama and he didn't want any part of it.

Juan caught a glimpse of Daryl leaving the scene and called out to him, "Yo Bro!"

Daryl turned and looked at Juan. Juan senior stood about 5'6", 160 pounds. He looked like he could be a gigolo with all the jewelry he was wearing. Juan removed the sunglasses from his face, stretched his arms out and shouted, "Jo, my friend. Joo don't gotta leave. I'm finito. Just make sure you use protection. She's a baby making machine, Papa." Juan laughed, placed his shades back on his face, turned and got back into the car with his friend.

The driver raised the volume in his miniature two-door sedan, grabbed a black revolver from the dashboard, passed it to Juan and sped off.

"I told you he's an asshole," said Marisol, rolling her eyes. She stopped at the sidewalk, crossed her arms and said, "You were just gonna leave me here all alone?" She sucked her teeth.

"I...I...I," Daryl didn't know what to say.

"Juan, Raoul!" shouted Marisol to her sons.

Her children stopped what they were doing and the elder Juan replied, "Que?"

"How many times I have to tell you not to say 'Que?' It's 'Yes, Mama,' Now you and tu hermanos come on. Ven aca!. We're going to la casa," she said, referring to their home.

Juan sucked his teeth. Though he was reluctant at first, his past punishment for disobeying his mother compelled him to comply.

Daryl stood still for a moment and studied the 5'1", 120 pound mami in her spandex and halter top. He'd heard stories about Spanish women gaining a lot of weight once they became pregnant. Had he not seen her three sons, he would have never believed they existed.

"You coming?" she asked, standing with one hand on her hip and the other caressing her thigh.

When Marisol moved, Daryl noticed the gap in between her legs. He looked over at her three boys, thought about how she had no problem inviting him back to her apartment and said to himself, "This is going to be an easy piece of ass."

Daryl complied with her request and walked with her back to her apartment.

At her place, Marisol straightened up her living quarters, cooked dinner for her children and sent them into their room to watch television.

Two DVD movies later, the kids were asleep and two of Daryl's fingers were buried deep inside Marisol's vagina. They French kissed as she humped his hand. She reached down to his pants and rubbed his crotch through his jeans. She looked at Daryl and said, "One second, Papa."

She got up, walked to her sons' bedroom and turned off their television. After rambling through their room, she turned off their light and closed the door. She walked over to the living room television and raised the volume a little bit and let her slip drop to the floor revealing swollen black nipples and a hairy vagina.

She sat on Daryl's lap and began kissing him again. She reached for his zipper and pulled his penis from his trousers. Marisol raised herself up and went to sit on Daryl's member when he stopped her. "Mami, hold up," he said pushing her back. "Let me get a condom first."

"Papi, no," she pleaded. "My coochie doesn't react very well to rubbers. So I take these now," said Marisol, reaching into her purse and pulling out several diaphragms with birth control pills in them. "I take them all because when I was on these," she said, holding up one of the diaphragms, "I still managed to have Little Juan. So now I take them all just in case."

"But Marisol…"

"Sshhh," she said, putting her finger on his lips. "For just a little while, Papi. Please, I need it. I no have no deek in long time," she whispered. She slid his member into her moist vagina and moaned. "I, Papi."

"Ooooh," said Daryl. Daryl didn't want to have unprotected sex with a woman he just met a few hours ago, but he couldn't help it. It felt too good inside of her.

She rode him like she hadn't had sex in years. With her screaming and one of her breasts being sucked on aggressively, Daryl's orgasm didn't take long to arrive. "Oh, shit," he yelled.

As soon as Marisol heard her cue, she grabbed Daryl's head and said, "Fuck me, Papi! Give it to me, Papi." It was a wrap after that.

Boom! Boom! Boom! Someone was banging at her door.

"Marisol! I know joo home, bitch. I am going to kill you when you open this door."

Boom! Boom! Boom! The guy continued to bang.

"Open this fucking door or I'll shoot right through it," he yelled.

Marisol jumped off of Daryl's lap and pulled him into her bedroom as he struggled to get his pants back up to his waist.

"Who the fuck is that banging on your door?" asked Daryl, nervously.

"It's Big Raoul. Just go!" she demanded.

The duo climbed over Marisol's twin bed that was supported by six crates and Marisol pulled open her window and said, "Go! Go!" with a wave of her hand.

As Daryl exited through the window, Marisol managed to grab onto his head and pull his face close to hers. She kissed him on his lips and said, "Don't forget about me, amigo."

Daryl climbed onto the fire escape and heard Marisol screaming out her telephone number like a commentator dictating a dog race. "5551927." Then she slammed the window behind him.

Ten minutes later, Daryl was on the New England Thruway heading home thinking about his previous episode. All sorts of crazy thoughts were entering his mind. *"What if she gave me an STD? Or what if she never took any of the birth control pills? Even worse, what if she was H.I.V. positive?"* Then he thought, *"What if crazy ass Raoul would've gotten inside that apartment and done a number on me? I'm bugging out!"*

A few months went by and Daryl's H.I.V. results came back negative. He was totally clean. He never did call Marisol and he told himself that he would never make love to anyone that he didn't know ever again without using a condom.

Today was Friday. Time to pick up little Daphne.

CHAPTER TWELVE

FRIDAY, CLUB NIGHT ...

Beep! Beep! Daryl was outside honking his horn.

Ring...ring...ring! My telephone was also ringing.

"I bet that's your father," I said, looking at Daphne while reaching for the telephone.

Little Daphne was always glued to the television set, watching one of her favorite cartoons, *Dora the Explorer* or *Sponge Bob*.

I picked up my cordless telephone and used my free hand to move the curtain to the side so that I could see who was honking their horn in front of my house.

"Hello," I answered in a measured tone. Looking from my window, I spotted Daryl's truck in my driveway.

"I'm outside, open your door," said Daryl, exiting his vehicle.

"It's already open."

Click.

I tossed the telephone on one of my two sofas and walked

back into my ground floor bathroom.

Daryl entered his former home just like he had been doing for the last two years. He'd walk in and head straight for the refrigerator. And ever since Daphne turned two years old, she looked forward to seeing her father every weekend and, as always, before he could make it to the kitchen, Daphne would run and jump into Daryl's arms and affectionately hug and kiss him.

"Mmtwa!" said Daryl, giving Daphne a peck on her cheek in return. "I love you too, Mamma," he said, as he returned his daughter to the ground. The little princess wasted no time finding her spot back in front of the television set.

Daryl walked into the kitchen, opened up the refrigerator and grabbed himself a beer. He then walked over to the bathroom where I was caught up unloosening the last few braids I had in my hair.

He peeked inside, "Hey, gorgeous." Then he took a sip of his beer.

"If this is what you call gorgeous, then I can imagine how sleezy those tramps look that you call yourself dating," I said, bringing my comb through my hair.

Daryl stared at me through the mirror. "So what's up?" he asked with a smile.

"Ain't nothing up, Daryl." I stopped combing to give my shoulders a rest and continued to talk to my ex-husband, looking at his reflection in the mirror. "You think you're slick."

"I loved it when you would say that to me." Daryl walked up behind me and wrapped his arms around my waist.

I pushed him off. "Stop, Daryl. I'm not fucking with you like that anymore. I'm tired of you thinking that you can come over here and fuck me every time you please like I'm one of your stupid whores." I rolled my eyes. I really didn't want to end our episodes, but something had to give.

"Did I ever say that you were a whore? And, I don't be trying to fuck you every time I come over here neither." He smiled, "Only sometimes."

"That's what I'm talking about, Daryl. That's exactly what I mean," I said, combing out another one of my micro braids. I stopped, turned around, looked at Daryl and said, "Look, tonight my friends and I are going out. We're going to the club."

"Well, go clubbing then." I guess Daryl didn't believe me.

"I am. And tonight I will finally get your stanking ass out of my system. I am going to find me somebody sweet who will appreciate me for me, and if he has any decency with him," I smiled devilishly, "he just might get some." I turned back toward the mirror and continued taking out my braids. Looking into the mirror, I returned my gaze to Daryl. *Any second now, his stupid ass ego is going to kick in.*

"So what, I'm supposed to be jealous or something now?" he asked with an envious look on his face.

"Nigga, ain't nobody trying to make your ass jealous," I said, wiggling my neck.

Daryl waved me off. "Yeah, whatever."

"I ain't," I said, leaning to the side to avoid a kiss that Daryl tried to plant on my neck. "Daryl, I'm moving on because I have a life, too. So, from now on, that shit is dead," I said, pointing toward the zipper on my pants. "No more playing games."

"Well, go ahead then, Mamma, do you!" Daryl turned and walked into the living room with an attitude.

"I am," I yelled.

"Listen, I'll call your ass tonight and make sure ain't no niggas up in here around my daughter's clothes and toys."

"You're not going to get an answer, Dee. I'm hanging out all night." I closed the bathroom door and sat down on the toilet to relieve myself.

Daryl scooped Daphne up off of the couch, ejected her animated movie from the DVD player, grabbed her bags and exited the house.

Against the advice of my family, friends and attorney, I was still secretly seeing Daryl. At least twice a month our divorced asses would have a 'quickie' and silently pray that we could one day work everything out. However, as soon as we would both reach our orgasms, all the things that we had come to dislike about one another would instantly pop up into our minds.

I kept condoms in my drawer for our numerous sexual encounters, plus I knew that he was a man and was probably running around town with anyone who'd drop their panties for him. On more than a few occasions, I'd hear gossip at the beauty salon about how Daryl was fucking this one or how this other one was sucking his thing dry, so I made it an effort not to have unprotected sex with him anymore.

Being a family oriented person, I was becoming uncomfortable with the sexual relationship Daryl and I were having. To me, it seemed to be based solely on sex or our daughter. Fed up, I decided that tonight would be the night I would find myself a man and get my life rolling again.

That evening, me, Kee Kee and a few of our other girlfriends all went out to a trendy night club that just recently reopened in downtown Manhattan.

My ass wore a black Dolce & Gabanna pants suit with a pair

of black Dolce & Gabanna boots. My hair was permed by my Dominican hairdresser and it was styled to hang low around my head, complimenting my makeup.

Kee Kee's outfit was a Prada skirt suit. Her jacket and bottom were cream and she touched it up with a pair of black six-inch Prada pumps.

The other three girls also wore designer threads. Danielle had on Gucci, Yvette wore Escada and Tanya had on Fendi.

Inside the club, we drew all the attention, as if we were the Jackson Five. Kee Kee knew she looked good and she expressed it by accepting a free round of drinks from a guy who looked like he was worth every bit of the expensive Armani suit that he wore.

While we were caught up in discussing which men looked good and which men we thought were gay, a tall attractive guy about 6'5", 220 pounds, tan complexion with dark curly hair walked up to the table and extended his hand out to me.

Danielle leaned over to Yvette and whispered, "Did God ever appear in the form of man because if he did, I finally got to see him."

"Shut up, girl," said Yvette. "I know one thing though, if he ain't God, then his ass must be Jesus." They both burst out in heavy laughter.

In his deep sexy voice, he introduced himself. "Good evening, ladies. How are you tonight?"

We all responded in unison. "Fine." If only he knew how horny we were.

"My name is Jerome and I couldn't help but wonder if you ladies would care for a drink?"

"Shoot 'em through," said Tanya, flirtingly.

"Fine, no problem. But first I'd like to know whether or not this fine specimen of a woman right here is single." He asked, looking into my eyes.

I blushed, returned the sexy gaze, noticed his platinum grey eyes and thought to myself, "This man will make some *beautiful babies*." Then I answered, "Yes, I'm single."

"May I have this dance then, madam?" he asked.

"Sure," I replied. Then he ordered a bottle of bubbly for our table.

We made our way to the dance floor and enjoyed entertaining one another for a few songs as well as getting to know each other.

Every now and again, I would look over at the table where my friends were sitting and receive tips and warnings that they would whisper to me.

Tanya said, "Don't let him touch your butt, girl."

"Touch his thing. See if he's huge down there," said Yvette, pointing toward Jerome's crotch area.

"He has a nice butt. A nice butt," mouthed Danielle.

When I looked over at Kee Kee, I mouthed to my good friend, "Kee Kee, what do you think?"

As we romantically rocked back and forth to a Luther Vandross hit, Kee Kee looked at me with a half drunken stare and said, "Fuck his ass tonight, Steph. And make sure he eats it," said Kee Kee, pointing down at my coochie.

I covered my mouth and laughed, causing Jerome to loosen up the clutch he had on me. Chuckling himself, he asked, "What, am I being goofy? Can I not dance or something?"

I leaned back and looked into Jerome's sexy eyes and said, "No, you can dance, baby. I just hope you're the one."

By the end of the evening, three of us had met guys that we were going home with. Kee Kee had her eyes set on a beautiful Dominican couple the entire night. Unfortunately, the wife wasn't into women or sharing her husband because Kee Kee tried unsuccessfully to seduce the woman in the restroom. Kee Kee and Tanya were the only two women out of our crew who would be either taking a cold shower that evening to cool down the heat or reacquainting themselves with a brand new pack of 'D' batteries.

The rest of us women scored, and I was the first one to leave and make my way to Jerome's house on 86th Street and Central Park West.

Inside his lavish apartment, everything was gold and brown. From the exquisite paintings down to his Persian rugs, a touch of gold or caramel fabric was stitched in perfectly.

I removed my jacket and accepted a drink that Jerome had prepared for me as we got comfortable on his living room love seat. The lights were dimmed and he and I chuckled over small conversation as we watched Jerome's exotic fish swim around in a large aquarium that sat in his dining room wall.

"So, are you enjoying yourself tonight, Stephanie?" he asked me.

I giggled. "Um hm." I brought the glass of champagne to my lips to take another sip but Jerome pulled my drink away. He grabbed me by the nape of my neck and gently pulled my face close to his. He stuck his tongue into my mouth and teased the inner folds of my jaw as his lips pressed softly against mine. He backed away after a few moments and led me to his bedroom. Up on the bed, our bodies came together again, with Jerome lying on top of me going through the motions of love making, only fully dressed.

I felt the hardness of Jerome's fully engorged penis as he humped up against me with every downstroke. My body raised strainingly to meet his every thrust as he put one hand on my breast and fondled my stiffened nipple through the thin material of my blouse.

Just when I thought Jerome would make a move and begin to undress me, his humps increased and he began talking dirty to me. "Come on, baby. Come for me. Let it go. Give it to me. You are so hot, Steph. Come on baby, come." He moaned as his humps increased in speed by the second.

I looked up at Jerome like he was crazy and thought, "I know this man is not trying to hump me on some first grade shit."

As soon as the thought left my mind, Jerome exploded into his trousers, giving off a loud moan in the process. "Ooooh, aagghhh!"

"Jerome!" I said, smacking his shoulder, unsure of what just happened.

He was exhausted. "Huh?"

"Did you just come in your pants?"

"Uh huh. It was great. Did you?"

"Hell no. Get your nasty ass up off of me," I shouted.

"What?" said Jerome, sitting up with a cum stain on his black cotton trousers.

"I don't believe this," I said, gathering my things.

"What, where are you going, honey? Wait!" said Jerome, trying to follow me to the door.

I grabbed my purse and jacket, walked to Jerome's door, opened it, looked back at him and said, "If I wanted a damn lap dance I would've hired a stripper." Then I slammed the door behind me. Nasty máfucka.

Jerome sighed, looked down at his stain soaked pants and thought, "Oh well, at least I got mine off."

CHAPTER THIRTEEN

To celebrate the ending of the summer season, Daryl, Tommy and Barry, another friend and coworker of theirs, flew out to South Beach, Miami for Labor Day weekend. The trio felt they deserved a vacation and, since it was Miami, they wanted to go all out and represent in style. The three stooges reserved a penthouse suite at the Shelbourne Hotel on Collins Avenue. They also rented a minivan, a yellow Lamborghini Roadster for $150 per day from Rent-a-Whip, and three mopeds from Motor-Peds, Inc. to assist them with their in-town travels.

Daryl pulled up and valet parked the sports car at the lobby of the hotel. He hopped on the elevator and quietly rode up to the top floor of the luxury establishment. When Daryl exited the elevator, he retrieved his key card from his front shorts pocket and slid the small piece of plastic into the door. When it clicked, he entered the rented suite and spotted a naked female dashing into one of the three bedrooms. A few seconds later, Barry exited the room smiling, dressed in only a pair of gym shorts and slippers.

Barry was about 6'5", 285 pounds. His skin was desert tan and he wore his hair in a big curly Afro. He was naturally strong and, although he wasn't as trim as his two friends were, he was quick and had beaten his comrades on more than one occasion in a friendly game of basketball. Indeed, he was a big fella, but his charm and sense of humor always attracted the ladies. And for whatever reason, they always came in abundance.

Daryl stopped and stood a few feet away from Barry and said, "Big man, what's happening? We just got here this morning." He smiled, leaned in closer to his friend and continued, "Who the hell was that that just ran into your room?" said Daryl, pointing at Barry's bedroom door.

Raising his hand above his shoulder and using his thumb to point behind him, Barry kept the grin on his face and replied, "Oh, that's a lil shorty I met in the lobby when I came back from picking up the Lamborghini. She's hot, too." Barry brought his hand back down and rested his thumbs in the waistband of his shorts.

"You fronting ass nigga," said Daryl, smiling harder now. He gave his friend a look that said, "You're the man," and then asked him, "What the fuck, you were hitting that on the couch or something?"

Barry slapped Daryl's hand as a gesture to say, "Yeah, I'm the man," and then said, "Nah, I ain't even hit shorty yet," said Barry, meaning that he hadn't had sex with the young lady yet.

Daryl frowned and said, "What? Well, what the hell were y'all doing? I know something was going down because I saw her little yellow bootie fly up in the room." They both laughed.

"We were playing hide and go seek," said Barry, still laughing.

Daryl paused and placed his hands on his waist. "Hide and go seek? What were y'all hiding, y'all's clothes or something?"

he asked.

"Nah, we were hiding from each other."

"Where the hell was she going to hide out here?" said Daryl, scanning the living room area.

"I was the one hiding, nigga."

Daryl placed his hand on Barry's shoulder and said, "Yo Bee, you're damn near 300 pounds. Where the fuck were you going to hide, with your big ass?" said Daryl, with a look on his face that told his friend, "Come on now, be for real."

"I was under the bed until you came in and scared ol' girl."

The duo looked at one another and burst out into heavy laughter. After a few moments, Daryl regained his composure and said, "Where's Tommy?"

"You know he had to check in with his wifey. His ass is at the store buying a bunch of calling cards." Laughing again, Barry gave his friend another slap on the hand and said, "Yo, lemme go and handle my business and I'll holla at you in a few, homie."

As Barry proceeded toward his room, Daryl cleared his throat causing his friend to stop and turn around. He asked, "Can I play?"

"You can play alright. Just dig your hand into your pants pocket," said Barry, pointing, "move it over to the side and grab that thing of yours that keeps getting you into trouble. Shake it like you're playing dice and when you crap out, holla at me." They both laughed again and Barry entered the room and went to handle his business.

Daryl figured since there wasn't anything else to do until later on, he might as well take a nap and catch up on his rest. Tired from the flight, Daryl walked into his designated room and went right to sleep.

LATER ON ...

Half asleep, Daryl tried frantically to swat the irritating bug that flew noisily around his head. When he opened his eyes, he noticed his two buddies standing over him giggling. Barry had one hand behind his back, hiding the strand of hair that he was using to agitate his tired coworker as he slept. As Daryl focused, he thought, "That wasn't no damn fly; that was Barry's ass playing." He jumped up and spat at Barry and Tommy. "Y'all niggas are always playing. Leave me the hell alone. I'm tired."

Daryl tried to turn over and use the quilt to cover his head, but Barry grabbed it and tugged on it, causing it to fall to the floor.

"Yo, Tommy, you see this shit. Ya man got on 'duh dun dah dunts,'" said Barry referring to Daryl's underwear and using a slowed down version of the theme music to Superman.

Daryl jumped up and grabbed a pair of shorts that he had lying nearby.

"Duh da da da duuhh, da da da duh dah duhn!" shouted Barry and Tommy in unison. They were mimicking the tune to Superman. The trio laughed as Daryl got dressed.

"Fuck y'all niggas," shouted Daryl as he entered the bathroom and proceeded to wash up.

Around 6 p.m. that evening, the threesome hit the strip on their rented motor scooters, cruising up and down Collins Avenue and Ocean Drive Boulevard. Whistling and cat calling, the two eligible bachelors brought along Tommy as they went looking for women to solicit.

At the light on 18th Street and Collins, a bright-colored

pickup truck sped by the group with a pack of women gathered in its rear cab. The women smiled, giving Daryl and Barry an invitation to flirt.

The trio revved their motors, giving the bikes all it had, until they caught the young ladies at the next light.

"Hey, mami," shouted Daryl to the small crew of Cuban sisters. Daryl lowered the sunglasses he wore to get a clearer view of his prey. In Miami, as long as you had on some type of eyewear to protect yourself from the bugs, you didn't need to wear a helmet.

The women waved back. "Where are y'all headed?" asked Daryl.

"Just riding," replied one of the girls.

"Tu tienes dinero, señor?" asked the passenger of the vehicle, looking Daryl up and down.

"Ayo, what did shorty say?" asked Barry. Barry was funny, but sometimes he could be as dumb as a doorknob.

"She said," answered one of the ladies in the rear of the 4x4, "if y'all got any money?" said the girl bashfully sticking her tongue out of her mouth.

"Hell, nah, we ain't got no money," said Tommy.

Daryl and Barry shot a look at Tommy that said, "Damn, homie, shut the fuck up." As soon as Moe and Larry looked at Curly, the truck pulled off taking the ladies with it.

The SUV disappeared in traffic and when the three amigos made it back to their hotel, they let Tommy have it.

"Yo, what the hell is wrong with you, Tommy, fucking up our pussy?" said Barry, sitting on his bike with the kickstand in position.

"Yeah, homie, cock blocking and shit," said Daryl, sitting

sideways on his bike.

"Pardon me, fellas, but y'all been riding me ever since we got out here." Tommy stepped off his bike and sat on a banister in front of the hotel.

"That's because you're tripping," said Barry.

"Tommy, look, I know how you are about your sweetheart and I know how you feel about people cheating, but look brah, Bee and I are single and we're just trying to have a good time. So, give us a break," said Daryl.

"My bad, my bad," said Tommy, walking up to his friends and giving them handshakes and hugs. "I am tripping because homegirl is all the way up top and she got me stressing. I should be here enjoying myself and instead, I'm ruining y'all's fun. Since I'm messing up y'all's groove, I apologize and I'll fall back. In fact," said Tommy, removing the key from his bike, "I'll be at the bar in the hotel till the wee hours of the morning, having a merry ol' time by myself. So basically, you two will have the room all to yourselves. Have fun," said Tommy, giving his friends another handshake and then walking into the hotel smiling.

Around ten o'clock that evening, Daryl and Barry hit the streets once again, this time in the Lamborghini. Up and down the streets of South Beach they drove accumulating telephone numbers as if they were working for the phone company.

"Meet us at the Shelbourne," said Daryl to a set of Philippine twins.

"Chow," said the girls simultaneously as they sat parallel to Daryl and Barry at the light in a cherry red Lamborghini Roadster.

The two gigolos spotted the two exotic ladies leaving a Taco Bell Drive-Thru and tailed them until they caught up with them at a nearby stoplight. There, the quartet exchanged smiles and conversation and came to the conclusion that the chicks were down for whatever as long as the price was right. And, if the ladies were going to fulfill their fantasies, then the guys would definitely have to pay for it.

At the room, Lu Lu and Lei Lei revealed to their customers that they were nineteen-year-old twins imported from their Asian country when they were just sixteen. They explained when asked about their taboo behavior that it was customary in their native land for two sisters to engage in sexual activity with the same man. The identical twins went on to further explain that any extracurricular activities that came about that evening were behaviors they picked up in Miami.

The twins were two perfectly proportioned copper-haired debutantes. They had large natural breasts and their rear ends had some firmness to them. The girls had small waists that they maintained through their vigorous workouts, and they were also just as enthusiastic about the encounter as Daryl and Barry were. The bill would run the guys $1,000, but for what they had planned, they felt it was worth it. There were no rules in their "anything goes" session and the ladies were theirs until the morning.

At the twins' request, the foursome gathered in the living room part of the penthouse and would perform their sexual antics lying beside one another.

"You two sit back and enjoy the show until we give you guys the signal to join in," said Lu Lu, stripping down to her garter belt and her red six-inch pumps.

"What the hell is our signal going to be?" asked Barry, impatiently.

"You'll recognize it when it comes," said Lei Lei, giving Barry a seductive wink as she stuck her forefinger into her mouth and slowly withdrew it.

For the next half hour, the sisters took turns on each other, exploring the inner folds of one another's sensitive labia. Lu Lu would feast on her sibling in one position, and when her kin would climax, positions would change and different erotic antics would take place with the other sister in control. After the girls pleasured one another, they got on all fours facing each other giving their male associates the signal to do what they did best.

When Barry entered Lu Lu, she grunted because he went up in her bunghole. He used a whole pack of condoms, stroking her vigorously in the same position. He only explored her vagina by finger.

Right across from him, Daryl received oral treatment for the second thirty minutes of their session, bringing him to his first orgasm. After he got up, went to the bathroom and urinated, his second climax arrived with Lei Lei riding him reverse cowgirl style. For his third eruption, Daryl laid Lei Lei on her stomach, lubed up her anus and reamed her into oblivion for forty-five minutes. When both teams were finished, Daryl set the alarm on his watch for 4 a.m., where he and his buddy woke up after two hours, switched partners and continued pleasuring themselves until 6:30 that morning.

Ten minutes to seven, the duo walked their dates to the lobby of the hotel where they found their friend Tommy sound asleep on one of the lounge sofas.

Barry yanked the pillow that supported Tommy's head from underneath him, startling his unconscious friend.

"Get yo ass up, nigga," said Barry with a mean look on his

face. "This ain't no homeless shelter. This is the…" and before he could get all of the words out of his mouth, he started to laugh, "Shelbourne. Where classy niggas sleep in penthouses and shit, not lobby couches."

Daryl laughed as Tommy proceeded to explain.

"I tried to make it to the elevator, but that gin I had last night jumped up out of my system, grabbed me by the hand and walked me over to this lovely sofa right here," said Tommy, fluffing up the pillows that he compressed by laying on them all night.

"Then what happened?" asked Barry, discreetly tapping Daryl as to say, "Listen to this crazy ass shit."

"Then that liquor his ass mixed with the gin came up out of nowhere and knocked his ass out," said Daryl, finishing the joke for his friend.

The threesome enjoyed a few more laughs as they shared their previous night's experiences with Tommy. Then, the trio ordered breakfast and had it sent up to their room. They were leaving that afternoon so they all went upstairs, showered, packed their belongings and began making phone calls to arrange a way to have their vehicles returned. Afterwards, the three man tag team made their way to the airport with one of them desperately eager to return home while the remaining two huffed and puffed about not reserving the room for one more day.

CHAPTER FOURTEEN

It was a warm Saturday afternoon and young Daphne was at Chuck-E-Cheese engaged in kiddie games along with some other children that were there celebrating birthdays or just spending quality time with their parents. Daryl was only a few feet away sitting in a corner discussing a blueprint layout with his good friend, Thomas. They had recently picked up a contract that M & M Construction outbid its competition for.

Meanwhile, on another side of the city, I decided to pay my parents a visit at their home in my old Brooklyn neighborhood. My parents still lived in the same brownstone they purchased a year before I was born.

As I pulled my car up to the curb, I noticed a small group of guys dressed in the latest Hip Hop fashions deeply involved in a street dice game called Cee-Lo. I kept my eyes glued to the small crowd as I grabbed my purse and exited the luxury vehicle. When my door slammed, the individual who was in control of the dice immediately paused and turned his attention toward me.

Antwan rattled the dice gently in his palm as he stared at my attractive figure. One of the guys kneeling down looked up at

Twany Two Gunz and quizzically asked, "Yo, Gunz, who's shorty right there that just pulled up on our set?" The guy nudged his head in my direction indicating that I was the subject of discussion.

Eighteen-year-old Antwan stood 5'8", 190 pounds. He kept his hair cut low, outlined it with long sharp sideburns and a trimmed mustache. He's a street kid who sells drugs on my old block and ever since he turned sixteen years old, he kept two 380 semi-automatic handguns on his person at all times. A few days after his sixteenth birthday, his older brother, Anthony, was gunned down in a gun battle when the eight-shot 9 millimeter he was carrying ran out of bullets granting his enemy the opportunity to ambush and kill him. When Anthony died, word quickly spread that if he had an extra firearm in his possession at the time of the shooting, he would've had no problem annihilating his rivalries. After Anthony was laid to rest, Antwan became the new thug on the block. And in an effort to prevent the same tragedy from happening to him, Antwan chose to always carry two guns on his waist. That's where he got the name Twany Two Gunz.

Antwan never took his eyes off of me. Without flinching, he confidently answered, "That's Stephanie, Mrs. Johnson's daughter."

"Big titty Steph that used to live..." and before Bernard could finish his remark, Antwan nudged him telling him to shut his mouth.

When I got within a few feet of the small mob, Antwan rose to his feet and spoke, "Hello, Stephanie."

I stopped at the bottom of the steps that led up to my mother's building, looked over at Antwan and pulled my designer sunglasses down to the brim of my nose. Unclear if it was him or not, I hesitantly replied, "Antwan, is that you?"

Twany Two Gunz smiled happily and anxiously walked over to my fascinating ass. Bashfully, he tucked his hands into his trouser pockets and said, "Yeah, it's me."

I returned the smile and said, "Wow, Antwan, you got so big. I remember when you were like twelve or thirteen years old. You were a puny little thing. Now look at you." I looked him up and down and continued to speak. "Wow, how are you, and how's your mother?"

He shrugged his shoulders. "She's fine. Everybody's doing really good." Antwan would always see me whenever I visited my parents' home. He also had a crush on me ever since he could remember, but never had the courage to tell me. He knew I had gotten married, and he also knew about my divorce.

Antwan found himself suddenly at the tip of the iceberg and the only direction to move was forward. As far as he was concerned, he was 'Twany Two Gunz', and if the hood didn't scare him, I couldn't either. When he realized I noticed him staring, he blushed again and continued to speak. "Stephanie, it is true what they say about you," he said matter-of-factly.

I changed my expression and automatically became serious. I adjusted the purse strap on my shoulder, fixed my glasses and with a puzzled look on my face I said, "Antwan, what is it that you done heard about me? Tell me what they're saying about me that you're agreeing with." I crossed my arms as I waited for a response.

Antwan's eyes darted back and forth as he tried to remain calm and focus on my hypnotic stare. Softly, he spoke. "That you have some beautiful eyes and some sexy ass lips." He smiled.

I let out a loud chuckle as my heart rate slowed down. I placed a hand on my chest signifying my relief, but when the comment sunk in, I didn't know what to say. "Antwan, how old are you?" I kindly asked.

Twan pulled his hands from his pockets and crossed his arms. His biceps were freshly tattooed and I caught a glimpse of a picture of a heart that had "I Love You Mom" written in red ink in the center of one of them. With a touch of confidence and an alarmingly deep voice, Antwan responded. "I'm eighteen, which makes me a man now. I'm responsible, respectful and I can take care of myself."

I wasn't sure where this was going, but I thought I had an idea. I wanted to be sure so I pressed Antwan a little more. "Antwan, who said my eyes were beautiful and that I had some sexy ass lips?" Again I folded my arms. I also forced a smile.

Keeping his cool, Antwan said, "I ain't the type to kiss and tell so I can't tell you who 'they' are." He emphasized the word "they" by holding up his hands and moving his index and middle fingers. He continued, "I also couldn't tell you why someone wouldn't want to spend the rest of his life with you right there by his side." He made the comment knowing that it would make me think about Daryl.

I blushed and softly said, "Aawww."

"But I can tell you this," he continued. He pulled a business card out of his pocket and handed it to me. "I can tell you why young men like myself go above and beyond the call of duty when it comes to pleasing older women like yourself."

To myself, I said, "Oh, really." However, I was impressed by the young man's approach so I took the card and looked at it. It read, "Antwan's Plumbing." It also had his pager number on it.

"Antwan, you do plumbing work or something?" I asked.

He smiled hard and said, "Well sort of, but basically I'm real good at laying pipe." He knew I'd get the joke. He prepared himself for rejection, but when I opened my handbag and dropped the card inside, he felt a tingle in his trousers.

I responded surprisingly, "You know something, Antwan? You're something else." I was smiling now. "I'll give you a call one day and if my drain is clogged, you better know how to fix it." Like Ninetendo, niggas keep some game.

Antwan smiled back at me. I then proceeded into my mother's building and Twan walked away adjusting the two guns he had tucked into his pants. He thought to himself, "I loves me some Stephanie."

CHAPTER FIFTEEN

When I entered my parents' home using the key I never discarded, I was immediately taken aback by the scrumptious aroma of my mother's gourmet cooking. The combination of meat and poultry such as baked ham, pork chops, roasted turkey and fried chicken along with the fresh garden smell of assorted vegetables including collard greens, green beans and boiled carrots brought me back to my days of childhood where a four-course meal came like the mailman, every day.

When I was born, my mother chose the traditional way of feeding which was simple, from her breast. But when my mom had to make an important appointment one day and leave little ole me with my father, when feeding time came, I wouldn't drink the breast milk that my mom squeezed into the bottle. So my dad emptied the contents out of the bottle and replaced my mother's fluid with some Similac and baby cereal. I devoured the meal and never looked back. As soon as my stomach was full, my fourteen-day-old ass burped and smiled proudly at my father as if to say, "Good looking out, Daddy. That's what I've been trying to tell Mommy all along."

My pops was as excited as any new father would be so he

placed the empty bottle on the living room table, cradled my precious little self in his strong arms, looked back down at me and said, "You shouldn't have been sucking on those things in the first place. That's my job." Then he smiled and when I saw my dad's pearly whites, I smiled back at him showing him my gums and securing the bond that would never be broken. When my mother learned of my new eating habits, she blamed my father for going against God's word and unsuccessfully tried to give me the titty over and over again. Defeated, my mom figured, "It's a done deal now. I guess I better get with the program." From then on, my eating habits always changed at my father's will.

At five months old, I was eating chicken from my father's plate. Seven months later when I turned one, I was eating chicken from my own plate. By the time I was eight years old, I knew the basics of preparing a meal and it made my mother extremely proud. Daddy, on the other hand, admired me for learning so many things at such an early age, but feared that if I cooked for someone else, that meant that I was grown and probably on my way to falling in love.

When I entered junior high school, my choice of recreation wasn't spending time with boys like my other teenage friends did. Instead, I buried my head in my books and focused on my future.

I wanted to be an accountant because I knew that it paid well, plus, my favorite subject was math. As time went on, I excelled academically and found myself working behind a cash register at a local supermarket. My girlfriends teased me about being a bookworm and indulging in so much work, but I never let it get to me. I may have been a young teenager, but I had my priorities straight.

Plenty of guys tried to court me, but I always turned them down. I figured at that age, with a small chest and a flat butt, I was unattractive and no one would want me for a girlfriend, only as a screwing partner, and I wasn't down for that. But when you're young, you're naïve and bound to slip sooner or later.

It was a few months after my sixteenth birthday and I was at work punching numbers and scanning items at my cash register. I rarely looked at my customers while scanning their items because I hated to lose count. So I'd wait until all of their items were totaled, then I'd look up and ask them if they were paying with cash or plastic.

One particular day, I was working register 2, the "Ten items or less" line. I remembered scanning ten items, so when I was approached with an eleventh, I knew I would have to decline the last item. When I looked up, what I saw was the cutest guy I thought I'd ever seen. He was tall, light skinned with natural jet black curly hair, a medium build and the sexiest voice. I was stuck for a moment. All I kept thinking was, "Why is he so cute? And why is he staring at me?"

My trance was broken when the latter of my questions was answered for me. In his deep baritone voice and killer smile that had me melting where I stood, the stranger who looked like a teenage fashion magazine model looked at me and said, "Stephanie, aren't you gonna scan my last item?"

The way he called my name made a feeling come over me that I had never experienced before. In between my legs began to moisten and I blushed uncontrollably. Just seeing his lips move threw me back into my trance and once again, the Barry White sound alike snapped me back into reality. "Aye, girl, you ain't gon scan my last item?"

Embarrassed, I covered my mouth. "Oh, I'm sorry. Hey, wait a minute," I said still smiling. "How'd you know my name was Stephanie?"

The guy pointed to my breast and said, "Your nametag."

I looked down and realized my name was etched across my left breast in big bold letters. I chuckled, then I said, "This line is for ten items or less, so I'm sorry to say that I can't process your last item."

"Not even if it's for you?" he asked flirtingly.

Beaming, I continued, "For me?" I looked down at the item and noticed that it was a box of chocolate covered cherries.

"Yeah," he said. "I think you should have these because they remind me of you."

"Now how do these chocolate covered cherries remind you of me and you don't even know me?" I placed my hand on my hip and anxiously waited for an answer. I worked the late night shift and not too many people shopped at that time. This allowed opportunities like the one underway to happen at any time.

"I'll tell you how," said the youngster clearing his throat. "You see, I never tasted these, but I know they're pleasurable. I also know that they're sweet on the inside and attractively smooth and chocolate on the outside." He paused so his words could sink in, then continued. "So what's it gonna be? You gon scan this last item and accept it as an invitation for a date or are you gonna decline it along with the idea of sitting beside me at the movies?"

Without hesitating, I scanned the eleventh item, bagged it, tucked it under my register so that I could grab it later, ripped the receipt from the cash register and wrote my name and telephone number down on the back of it.

When the weekend arrived, we found ourselves sitting in the parking lot behind a movie theater alongside a bunch of other young horny couples. The movie was good, but my date and I, whom I'd come to know as Rodney, were anxious to leave so we could cuddle up and make out like the rest of the kids our age were doing.

Rodney slid over to the passenger side where I sat and pressed his soft lips up against mine. I allowed his tongue to enter my mouth and we enjoyed every minute of the tongue game. Rodney touched me all over and when I didn't move his hand away from my crotch area, he took it as a cue to move forward. Rodney reached over to his glove compartment keeping his tongue buried inside of my mouth, opened it and pulled out a box of condoms. He released his grip and said, "Do you feel like doing it?" He showed me the box of rubbers.

I sat up, looked around at all of the other cars with their fogged up windows and thought, "It's finally going to happen." Then I looked back at Rodney and said, "Does this mean you're my boyfriend?"

Playing the role, Rodney leaned back over to the driver's side of the car, looked into the rearview mirror as if he were talking to the vehicle behind him and said, "Here you go with this shit." His profanity startled me but in a strange way, it also turned me on because it made Rodney seem like a mature adult. "We drive all the way out here and then you start fronting." He looked at me.

"I'm sorry," I said, "but I just thought..."

He cut me off. "You just thought what?" He raised his voice, sighed, then regained his composure. "Listen, I'm sorry, Stephanie. I didn't mean to force you or anything like that and

I don't know if you could be my girlfriend, especially if you're gonna be fronting on me. You told me you were a virgin and what if I hit it and it ain't tight. Then I'll figure you were lying to me all along. Then we'd be finished all together. But if you let me see for myself first, then I can make my decision." Rodney looked back into the rearview mirror, then into the side view mirror on his side. He thought to himself, *"In about thirty seconds, shorty is going to give in; they always do."* He reached for the keys in the ignition as if to start the car, looked back over at me and said, "What's up?"

I pulled his hand away from the ignition, rolled my eyes and leaned back into the seat. I lifted my buttocks from the chair, raised my skirt, slid my panties down to my ankles, pulled them off, rolled my eyes and shyly said, "Come on. Be gentle though."

The whole thing lasted no more than two minutes. About thirty seconds to fit himself all the way into my vagina and about ninety seconds of humping. Rodney was satisfied while I wondered if I had a boyfriend or not. But as the weeks went by and no word from Rodney, I knew that I had played myself. Instead of crying over it, I buried myself deeper into my books and continued admiring guys from a distance until the one I desired the most approached me one day at my church.

"Hey, darling," said my mother, draped in her favorite cooking apron. I entered my mother's home and hung my pocketbook up on the empty coat rack.

"Something smells good in here. You cooking for somebody special, Mom?" I asked already knowing the answer. I was in the kitchen now standing beside my mother.

My mom waved her hand playfully, grabbed a potholder

and pulled the roasted turkey from the oven. She said, "You know I always cook when my baby comes over. And where's that grown granddaughter of mine?"

I had my own apron on by now and was helping my mother set the table. "She's with her father." My mom sucked her teeth. "Maaah! Just because Daryl and I didn't last like you and Daddy doesn't mean that he's a bad person." I reached for the candied yams.

My mother checked her greens. "I still think y'all should've worked it out."

"Hey, there she is," my father said entering the kitchen. He returned from the corner store after purchasing some beverages. He and I embraced one another, and when my dad let go, he leaned over and peeked into the pot where my mom was checking the greens. He asked, "Is the food ready yet?"

My mother tapped his hand and said, "Sit down, would you."

I stuck my cheek out letting my father kiss me before he retreated back into the living room to watch a football game.

"You know, Cynthia is having a cookout this Sunday. She told me to tell you to come by," said my mother getting some cups from out of the cabinet.

"She did?" I said licking my fingers as I spread food throughout the three plates. "How is she?"

"That girl is as big as a house," replied my mother.

"I wonder if Daryl knows," I said. "Come on, Daddy, your food is going to get cold," I yelled.

"He oughtta know – it's his cousin," my mother rolled her eyes.

"Yeah, Mom, that's my girl though. I'll give her a call later and let her know I wouldn't miss it for the world. Come on, come on," I said wiping my hands clean on my apron. My mom and dad sat down at the table and joined me as I said a quick prayer. "God, thank you for allowing us this opportunity to get together today to have this meal. We thank you for the blessings you've bestowed upon us over the years and we ask that you watch over us continually, and guide us down the straight path. We thank you Lord and we're forever grateful." We all said Amen and dug into our food like there was no tomorrow.

I couldn't wait to go over to Cynthia's for the cookout. Her get togethers were always the bomb, and always full of surprises.

CHAPTER SIXTEEN

The following afternoon, I was driving home listening to my *Carl Thomas* CD, tapping on my steering wheel with my fingers as I grooved to the heartfelt tunes of the artist's first single, *Emotional*. I stopped at a red light and bobbed my head until the light turned green. As I slowly began to accelerate, I spotted a group of young guys rolling dice on the sidewalk and instantly thought about Twany Two Gunz. "I wonder what he's up to," I thought. "I think it's a shame how these kids are out here ruining their lives on these dag on street corners." My thoughts continued causing me to reach over to the center console of my sedan, remove the card that read, "Antwan's Plumbing" from my pocketbook, press the power button on my mobile phone, then press speaker and dial the number. There was a single ring, then three loud beeps.

Ring...beep, beep, beep.

I entered my mobile phone number and pressed the "End" button. Within minutes my phone was ringing.

Ring...ring...ring!

I smiled at the young man's promptness then pressed the "Talk" button.

"Hello," I said as I lowered the volume on my stereo.

"Yo, who dis?" asked Antwan. The unfamiliar number had him puzzled.

"It's me, Stephanie." I eased my way onto the ramp entering the highway.

Antwan smiled, lowered his head and quietly strolled away from the small group of guys who were entertaining themselves with neighborhood war stories.

I didn't hear anything for a short moment. I thought that we may have gotten disconnected so I called out again just in case. "Hello, Antwan?" The way I called his name made his head swell up, in both places.

"Yo, I'm here. I'm just buggin' that you decided to call me, na mean." Twan wasn't shy, but speaking with me made him feel awkward. He continued walking down the block to gain some privacy as our conversation proceeded.

"Well, it's always a pleasure lending a few kind words to a friend." I switched to the center lane and placed my vehicle on cruise control. The speed limit was sixty-five. I locked in at 70 m.p.h.

Twan stopped and leaned on a parked car. "So what's up with you? What made you call me?"

"I was thinking about you."

He smiled, "Oh, word."

"Yeah, I was wondering, are you going to school or anything, Antwan?"

"I'm saying I'm a go. I'm just trying to stack some paper right now." He looked at the diamond encrusted Bulova watch that he recently purchased from a crackhead.

"Well try not to waste too much time out there in those

streets. Too many of our young brothers are losing their lives out there, getting caught up with all of that fast money."

"I know. I'm a be ahight though."

I sighed and shook my head, "If you say so."

"So what's up with you? What are you doing this weekend?" Antwan was now admiring the diamonds in his pinky ring.

"I'm going to a cookout." I quickly glanced over my shoulder to make sure no cars were coming on my right side. When I saw that the coast was clear, I put on my right turn signal, drifted over to the right lane and prepared to exit on the next ramp. "You know Cynthia, right?" I asked.

"Who, Daryl's cousin?" Twan had a smirk on his face.

"Uh hm. She's having a cookout this weekend. She invited me so I'll be over there all day Sunday." When I exited the expressway, I noticed a patrol car parked at the corner with its dome light illuminated. I was the only car approaching the intersection and I knew about the police issuing tickets to drivers who operated their vehicles while talking on their cellular phones. "Listen, Antwan, I'll have to call you some other time. The cops are out here and I can't afford a ticket right about now from talking on my phone while I'm driving. So I'll talk to you later. Okay, sweety?"

"Ahight, Boo. Holla at me."

Click. I ended the call and never realized that Antwan called me Boo.

Antwan closed his cell phone, leaned his elbows on the roof of the car and allowed his mind to roam to a time when his older brother kicked some game about baggin' women.

"Listen here, lil brah." The two of them were at home sit-

ting on Anthony's bed in the room they both shared at their
mother's apartment. Anthony was counting his money and would
pass it to Antwan to rubber band up as he lectured his younger
sibling about the ladies. "When you want a chick, you go all out
to get her."

"You mean…"

Anthony cut him off. "Just listen. Damn! Hardheaded niggaz
never learn 'cause they don't listen. You have ta listen sometimes."

"Okay, okay."

"Now, bitches like to know that their man is a man's man.
Not no pussy ass nigga. You need to be tough. Not too thugged
out but rough enough where the bitch is going to feel safe around
you. You have to carry yaself in a way that you command respect.
You let the bitch know you're the boss without beating on her.
You let her know that you have the power. That you're the autho-
rative figure in the situation, that you're in control. But don't be
too arrogant wit it. Be confident about your manhood. Show
that bitch who's boss in every situation even if you have to
chump the next man in front of her. You never do no corny shit
like fight over a bitch, but if a nigga is playing himself and tryna
violate and you know shorty belongs to you, be the nigga that you
are. The man that she expects you to be and handle ya bidness
like a real nigga would. Straight up, do you! And from that point
on, the bitch will know where her place is and will *always* stay
in line. Trust me."

Twan sat there thinking, "She called me sweety, so I must
be her nigga. As soon as I get the chance, I'll show her who's the
man." Twan responded to his pager that was vibrating on his hip.
He removed it from his belt, brought it up to his face, looked at

the number and said, "A fuckin' fiend," then he made his way back down the block.

CHAPTER SEVENTEEN

Ring...ring...ring!

Daphne heard the telephone ringing, sprang up from her Indian style sitting position in front of the television and ran towards the telephone screaming, "I got it, I got it."

At the same time, I was also rushing for the phone, looking at my daughter who was shouting that she'd answer it. I said to myself "Sit your ass down," then aloud, "Sit your butt down girl. I got it." I arrived at the location first, picked up the phone, said hello and looked at Daphne who was walking away with her arms crossed, cheeks puffed out, attitude in full swing.

The person on the other end responded, "Yo, what's up?" It was Daryl.

I tucked the phone under my ear using the support of my shoulder and walked back into the kitchen. I answered, "Cooking." I switched ears and continued stirring my chicken stew.

"What cha cooking?" he asked.

"Some chicken stew, why?"

"'Cause I haven't eaten yet."

"Well I'm only cooking enough for Daphne and myself so

you're outta luck, Dee."

"Where's my little princess anyway?" Daryl was at home in his bedroom watching *SportsCenter* with the volume on mute.

"Let me tell you." I stuck my cooking spoon into the stew, drew it to my lips, tasted it and whispered to myself, "more pepper." Then I continued with my conversation. "Don't you know little 'grown ass' ran to the phone when it rang a little while ago like the phone was for her." I peeked in the living room and when Daphne noticed me, she crossed her arms, rolled her eyes and said, "Stop saying bad words, Mommy."

Daryl heard her and chuckled softly. "See what I mean? You think it's funny? With her grown ass," I said.

"You know who she gets that from, right?" asked Daryl.

"You, and your side of the family," I said with a shimmy of my neck.

"Let me speak to her." He flicked the channel to *ESPN 2*.

"Hold on." I pulled the phone from my ear and yelled, "Daphne!"

To my surprise, Daphne responded by saying, "I'm watching TV." She still had her attitude.

"Girl, if you don't get your butt over here right now and talk to your father..."

Daphne didn't even hear the remainder of the sentence. She jumped up, ran into the kitchen, grabbed the phone from me, placed it under her ear mimicking her Ma Dukes, placed her free hand on her hip like she was grown and said, "Yes, Daddy."

"That's a damn shame!" I said to Daphne who was exiting the kitchen.

"How's my little princess?" said Daryl in a childlike voice.

He rolled over on his back and looked toward the ceiling.

"Fine," responded Daphne bashfully. She made her way to the sofa and took a seat.

"I miss you." Daryl's voice was sweet and sincere.

"I miss you too, Daddy."

"I love you."

"I love you too, Daddy. Daddy?" she asked.

"Yes, sweetheart." Daphne's voice always made Daryl's heart melt. He rolled back on his stomach and switched the channel back to *SportsCenter*.

"Um...um," Daphne was excited to speak with her father and whenever she got that way, she stuttered. Daryl always made her laugh and spoiled her as much as he could "I'm watching Sponge Bob, and...and Sponge Bob is going like this," Daphne spun around in circles demonstrating as if her father could see her.

Daryl smiled and played it off, "For real?"

"Um, hmm." She sat back down.

"You want to come with Daddy to Aunt Cynthia's house this weekend?"

"Um, hmm." The way Daphne felt about her father, she would've agreed to go to the moon with him had he asked her to.

"Okay, now ask Mommy can you go with Daddy to Aunt Cynthia's house for a cookout this Sunday."

Daphne walked into the kitchen while Daryl was talking to her and said, "Mommy, um...um..."

"Slow down, breathe," I said aware that Daryl kept Daphne excited at all times.

"Daddy said to come to Aunt Cynthia's house to eat."

"On Sunday," said Daryl into the phone smiling from ear to ear. He imagined the sweet, innocent look Daphne had sprawled across her face as she tried to explain the situation to her mother.

"On Sunday, Mommy."

"Lemme see that phone," I said reaching for my cordless telephone.

Daphne pulled it back and as I struggled with her for it, Daphne quickly said into the receiver, "I love you, Daddy," before I pulled it away.

"I love you too."

"I miss you, Daddy, mmtwa!" He heard her kiss him and when he kissed her back, I was already on the phone.

"Was that for me?" I asked playfully.

"No." I sucked my teeth. Daryl continued. "Yours would've been sloppier, with a little bit of tongue mixed in there." He smiled.

I giggled. "I spoke to your cousin the other day and she told me about the cookout too. She said that I should come to her little ghetto get together and to bring Daphne, but since she's already going with *you*," I said sarcastically, "I guess I'll be traveling alone."

"Well, we'll see you up there then. No big deal."

"Whatever, you and your daughter are something else. But I'll be there. She said I could bring Kee Kee and them too."

"Do she still be going over to your mother's house?" asked Daryl.

"They live right next door to one another. She practically lives over there. I think my dad likes her too, because he's always showing off when she's around."

"Don't be trying to stay related to me through your dad

and my cousin," said Daryl smiling.

I sang like an old Big Pun and Joe tune, "Don't nobody wanna be a Manning no more." I stuck my tongue out.

"I see you still kept my name though."

"Whatever. I just like the way Manning sounds," I smiled.

"Yeah, ahight, you like the sound of the mailman ringing your doorbell every month with that alimony check in his hand. That's what's up."

"Boy, please, I don't need your dag on money." I waved my hand.

"So give it back then," said Daryl half playing and half serious.

"Listen, Dee, this stew is done. I'm about to fix your daughter's plate, make mine and take a nap. We'll speak to you later."

He sighed, "Ahight, Steph, love you."

"I love you too, Dee."

"Kiss Daphne for me."

"I will."

"Aight then, later."

"Bye."

Click.

I entered my living room, laid the phone down, walked over to Daphne and said, "Sweety, Daddy told me to give you a kiss."

Daphne leaned over and let me place a kiss on her cheek. When I backed off, Daphne said, "Wait, Mommy." She turned her other cheek in the direction of my face and said, "Give me a kiss for you." I smiled and placed a peck on Daphne's other cheek. Then Daphne said, "I love you, Mommy."

"I love you too," I said. I turned, walked into the kitchen and proceeded to make Daphne a bowl of my chicken stew.

CHAPTER EIGHTEEN

BROOKLYN, NEW YORK
THE COOKOUT ...

"**S**ingle ladies, I can't hear you! Single ladies, make noise! Single ladies, I can't hear you! Single ladies, make noise! All my independent women put yo hands up! Put yo hands up, put you hands up!" screamed the infamous nightclub DJ, Fat Man Scoop over a mixtape. His voice could be heard up and down the entire block as it blared from the numerous speakers that lined the outer fence of Cynthia's backyard. "I ne-ver knew there was a, love like this before." Faith followed up in her strong sultry voice. The place was jam packed.

Everybody from the neighborhood was in the house. Cynthia's younger sister, Sharon, stood guard at the door accepting the two dollar admission fee it took to enter the gathering while Cynthia herself made her way around the party tending to her house guests.

Sharon was the crazy one. Clad in a pair of house shoes, cut off jean shorts and a red tank top, she allowed her breasts to bounce up and down every time she moved as more and more people showed up.

"Two dollars," said Sharon holding her hand out to a female guest. The female rolled her eyes and paid Sharon in coins.

"Wait, nigga!" said Sharon leaning her 120 pound, 5'2" frame to her right side. She gently placed her hand on the subject preventing him from entering the premises.

"Wait for what?" said Twany Two Gunz who was accompanied by two of his friends.

"Yeah, wait for what?" asked Bernard, Twan's right-hand man. Bernard was a follower, Twan's "yes man."

"Where's my money?" Sharon had her hand out while her other hand rested on her hip clutching a bunch of singles.

"How much is it to get in?" asked Twan.

"Two dollars, and since it's three of y'all, and y'all out there selling drugs all day long, you might as well give me a ten dollar bill."

"Ayo, Son," said Twan, looking over his shoulder at Bernard, "give Sharon's ass a twenty dollar bill and let her keep the change. Her ass probably need it anyway, charging niggas and shit." He looked back at her. Then looked her up and down.

"Nigga, you supposed to be a hustler and shit. Twenty dollars shouldn't hurt you. If your brother, Anthony, was alive, he would've showed me mad love."

"That's 'cause he was fucking you."

Sharon threw up her hand and gave it a funky twist, then she said, "Yeah, whateva, just give me the money so I can let y'all in."

Twan looked at Bernard's hand and said, "Give it to her, Son."

Bernard handed Sharon the money and she let the trio enter hoping that they wouldn't start any trouble.

Twan was right. His brother, Anthony, *was* fucking Sharon before he died. Sharon wanted to surprise Anthony and tell him that she was pregnant, but when she rushed home with the news, Anthony was already dead.

Sharon was so stressed that she miscarried at Anthony's wake. She told her sister that it was just her period, that because of all the drama, she was careless and forgot to wear a tampon. In her heart, she knew that God had caused it to happen for a reason only He knew. Her logic was, "No child should be brought into this world without a father. The next time I get pregnant, that nigga is gonna be alive and kicking for his kid."

In the backyard where all the partying was taking place, Daryl, myself, Tommy, Barry, Kee Kee and the gang along with about forty other people were doing the Electric Slide to *Faith's* and The Fat Man Scoop's duet.

"Go, Daryl, go, Daryl, go, Daryl, it's your birthday!" A large group of party goers were gathered around Daryl singing as he playfully displayed his dance moves. He went from doing the Electric Slide, to The Cabbage Patch, to The Wop, then he broke it down and two-stepped his way to the nearest beer.

Tommy handed Daryl a cold bottle of Heineken and said, "Go, Daryl, do the crackhead, go, Daryl, do the crackhead!" They both laughed.

"Yo, have you seen Barry?" asked Daryl, giving his friend a handshake that ended with a snap of their fingers.

Tommy raised his hand that clutched the beer, motioned with it and said, "I think he's over there doing The Hustle."

Daryl looked in the direction where Tommy was pointing

and saw Barry shaking his big ass like he had no worries in the world. Daryl laughed.

"Daryl, is Sharon your first or second cousin?" asked Tommy. Tommy was up to something and Daryl sensed it.

"She's my first cousin, Tommy. She's only twenty-one and she likes single men. Anything else?" he asked, looking Tommy square in the eyes.

"Damn nigga. I'm only twenty-six. Plus, I'm getting tired of Karen's nagging ass." Tommy's facial expression showed signs of pain and sorrow.

Daryl gave Tommy a bewildered look. "Tommy? Tired of Karen? Since when, Mr. Loverboy?"

Tommy sighed, "I'm saying, Dee, we just haven't been clicking lately. I come home, eat and go right to sleep. And she don't say anything. If she ain't reading one of her books by that *Antoine Thomas* cat, then she on the phone with one of her friends."

"Damn kid, it's like that?" Daryl tried to empathize.

"It's all good though."

"Have y'all been out on the town lately, cooked for her, gave her a massage, flowers, anything?"

"I want to, but I be too tired, Dee."

"Take some time off, nigga. Me and the crew can handle things at the job. Go ahead, handle your household business. Never could I allow you to just let your relationship go, especially seeing how my separation had me fucked up. I'm telling you, Tommy, your ass won't be able to eat, sleep, you'll be twisting and turning all night, jacking off, running back and forth to the bathroom with the runs. Breaking up is serious when you're in love." They laughed, but Daryl was serious. He didn't want his friend to end up sad and lonely like he was.

"Ahight then, Dee. I'll take some time off. Probably take Karen on a vacation or something. She deserves it with all the stress she's been under at work and all. Good looking out, partner."

"Any time." He gave Tommy a pat on his back.

Tommy was pondering in his head what he'd do special to spark things back up at home. He looked up and noticed something. He saw me arguing with someone.

"Antwan, get off of me!" I shrugged Twan's hand from my shoulder.

THREE HOURS EARLIER ...

"Ayo, son, I only got like 10 nickels left. This crackhead nigga right here wants 20 for $85." Twan's lil man was standing on the second step of the brownstone building that Twan lived in. This made the 15-year-old the same height as the lanky drug addict.

Twan got up from where he was sitting on the hood of a car parked directly in front of his building, reached into the crack of his ass, grabbed the small sandwich bag that held 50 more slabs of crack, handed his worker 10 more nickels, cheeked the rest of the work, then resumed his position.

The crackhead waited for Nard to count up the money, and when he received a nod confirming his approval to get ghost, the fiend nodded back, turned, looked at Twan and said, "Thank you, Twan. You're alright." The two remaining teeth he had in his mouth twinkled from the sunlight as he spoke.

"Yo, Twan," Nard spoke nervously, "is that $15 gonna come out of my..." Twan cut him off. But not before the horn of the late model vehicle that just pulled up to the curb caught his attention.

"Nard, just shut the…"

Beep…Beep…Beep.

Twan turned to see who it was that was pulling up on his set. At the same time, his hands clutched his two guns.

I rolled my passenger side window down, crouched down just a bit to get a good look at Twan, then thought to myself, "I must be crazy, because his young ass damn sure looks good today."

"Antwan, what are you gonna do, stand there and stare at me or come over here and holla at a sistah?" I was looking sexy as hell too behind the wheel of my car.

"I love a chick with her own shit," thought Twan. Slowly, he walked over to my car and leaned into the window. As his elbows rested on the passenger side window pane, Twan looked to his left, he looked to his right, then looked out the driver's side window over my head, and when he figured that the coast was clear, our conversation began. "What choo doing in this here neck of the woods?" he asked. Twan tried to look charming. I noticed it and thought that it was cute.

"I just stopped by to say hello." I shifted my gear into park.

"Well hello to you too." Twan was beaming.

I peered over my steering wheel, looked back at Twan and said, "You wanna go for a ride?"

"Where to?"

"Junior's. I'm in the mood for something sweet." I smiled seductively at Twan.

Instantly, Twan's dick got hard. "Well what do you need to go to Junior's for? Sugar Daddy is right here." Twan laughed at his own joke. So I joined him.

"So are you coming or what?"

Twan thought about it for a second, then said to himself, "I got beef with some niggas on Flatbush Avenue and some niggas on Dekalb. Fuck it though, I'm Twany Two Gunz. If some shit pops off, then me and ole girl are gonna have to Bonnie and Clyde it through the whole downtown side of Brooklyn together." Twan swallowed his thoughts, opened the door and hopped inside the whip.

"Buckle up, big boy, safety first," I said.

Six songs and 15 minutes of commercials and advertisements later, Twan and I were seated at a table in the restaurant. Sitting across from one another, Twan sipped on a large soft drink while I stabbed at my dessert.

"So let me ask you," I looked into Twan's brown eyes and I kept my fork busy with the cream filled appetizer. "With all of these nice looking young ladies all around you to choose from, what makes you interested in older women?"

Twan adjusted himself in his seat. "I wouldn't say that I'm interested in older women altogether, it's just that I've always had a crush on you, Stephanie."

"Is that so?" I was surprised. Looking back now, I still didn't see where it seemed as though Twan was interested in me. But then again, it was never a thought of mine so I never really looked for any signs anyway.

"Hell, yeah, I mean shit, you look mad good, Steph. You're beautiful, your body is off the hook. You're working, you got your own whip and you got dough." Twan sipped on his drink.

I chuckled, "What makes you think that I have money, Antwan?"

"You invited me out for dessert, so I know you got some paper." We both laughed.

"Oh, you got jokes now," I said.

Twan pointed his right index finger at me as if to say, "Yeah, I got your ass, didn't I?" Then he said, "Nah, I got the bill. I wouldn't be a gentleman if I didn't pay for our lil date."

"So this is a date, huh?" I asked.

"If you want it to be," said Twan, half serious.

"A date it is then." I raised my bottle of water and met up with Twan's soda which was also raised for a toast.

"To our first," I said. The two containers touched.

"To our first, and may we have many more," said Antwan.

I took a few swigs of my water while Twan sipped casually on his drink. Our eyes remained locked on one another's for the next few moments. Afterwards, we got up and exited the eatery.

When I dropped Twan back off at his building, we both said our goodbyes and I told him that I would call him later.

Just a few hours ago, everything was all good. Now, the scene was like something out of a movie, and things only seemed like they were going to get worse.

"I thought you was gonna call me. I thought I was yo man." Twan was making a scene. He figured Daryl would step up. In fact, he hoped for it, that way, I could see who the real man was after all.

Daryl and Tommy ran to my aid. "Yo, what's going on? Twan, what's up?" Daryl looked back and forth at me and at Twany Two Gunz. Neither of us answered. He then focused in on me. "What's up, Steph?"

"Nothing, I'm alright." I looked at Antwan. "I think you should leave." My arms were folded and I was tapping one of my feet.

"Leave? I paid just like everybody else up in this bitch. I ain't going nowhere!" Antwan changed his facial expression to make it seem like he was the hardest nigga in the world.

Daryl stepped in closer to Twan and said, "Twan, she said leave."

Twan backed up and pulled out his two guns causing the music and everyone dancing to it to stop. "Now we really gon party," said Twan waving the pistols recklessly.

"Whoa, whoa! Be easy, champ," said Tommy backing up. Daryl remained silent and didn't move.

I brought my hand up to my mouth, but was too shocked to scream.

Barry made his way through the crowd and asked Daryl, "Yo, Dee, what's up?" Everyone was still. Barry looked at Daryl, then at Tommy, then at me and finally, he locked eyes with Twan.

"Fuck is you looking at big man?" Twan raised both of his guns and pointed them at Barry's head. He was swaying nervously side to side. Barry raised his hands slowly to face level as if to protect himself from any incoming bullets. He looked at Twan and swallowed hard.

"Antwan, just leave!" I screamed.

"Shut the fuck up, you lying bitch! You said you was gonna call me."

When Twan cursed at me, he lowered one of his weapons. By this time, Sharon was on the phone dialing 9-1-1. Daryl tried to make a move but froze when Antwan raised the other gun to my face. Twan had one gun pointed at Barry and the other gun pointed at me. He looked at Daryl and said, "What, what you gonna do now, *Superman*?"

Daryl half sighed but was stuck for words.

"How about I make your decision for you," said Twan. He then went from my face with the gun and brought it to Daryl's chest. I looked as if I was about to vomit right there on the spot.

In the far distance, we all heard sirens screaming as squad cars raced to the scene. For a minute, Antwan thought about the day he'd seen his brother dead on the ground. The police weren't even courteous enough to cover up his body with anything. They just stood there and waited for the coroner to arrive. It was the medics from the ambulance who finally covered Anthony up. Inside his head, Antwan heard the shots that killed his brother. He jerked and squeezed the triggers on both of his pistols by accident. Barry took one to the stomach and dropped to his knees, then to the floor. Daryl got hit in the chest and instantly fell backwards. Sharon screamed, "Aaagghh!"

I screamed too, "Aaagghh!"

The place went into a frenzy after that. The turntables got knocked over. Guys were climbing speakers and hopping over fences. Twan made it out though. But someone spotted him run and climb into an abandoned building and alerted the cops. While the police surrounded the premises, I was crying frantically over Daryl's dying body in the back of an ambulance.

On a bullhorn, a police sergeant called out to Twan. Two teams of police were lined up on either side of what used to be the front door where Twan entered just moments ago. "Antwan Fuller, we know you're in there. We have the place surrounded. Come out with your hands up!"

To himself, Antwan whispered, "I thought they only said

shit like that in the movies." He chuckled as a tear appeared in his eye.

A few tense minutes went by and there was no response from the suspect. Twan was inside preparing to surrender when the sergeant spoke up again. "Antwan Fuller, you're surrounded. Nobody's going to hurt you. Toss your weapons out the window and come out with your hands above your head or we're going to come in there and get you!" Twan took a deep breath, emptied the bullets except for one onto the floor and slowly crawled toward the door. "I ain't trying to suffer in no jail, fuck them," thought Twan.

The firing squad had their ear plugs in and one of the marksmen thought he was told to go in. He nudged his partner and when the officer took off, his crew followed.

What happened next is still a mystery. One shot was fired, and inside of the building a spark flashed making it light up like a lightning storm seconds after the officers entered. Spectators heard shouting and a popping sound. One minute later, an officer exited the building holding his hand up signaling to his other officers that the standoff was over. The officer removed his safety helmet, sighed, wiped his brow and said, "Sergeant, the suspect is down, he's dead." The kid's death was a mystery. The police reported that Antwan died by a self-inflicted wound. The streets, on the other hand, knew that the police were crooked so they came up with their own conclusion. The cops killed him. Simple as that.

Daryl and Barry were raced to Kings County Hospital and immediately rushed into surgery. Crime scene officers combed the vicinity of Cynthia's home while investigators spoke to witnesses and gathered evidence. For a second time, Mrs. Fuller was delivered the tragic news that one of her sons had been shot and killed, only this time, possibly by the hands of New York City's Finest. Mrs. Fuller cried, but her tears wouldn't fall. She didn't have the strength, and she didn't have to worry anymore either. No more jumping when gunshots were fired in her neighborhood, no more cringing up when police sirens raced past her window, and no more waiting by the telephone for that crying voice on the other end telling her that her only surviving son was killed. The call was made face to face by a nosy neighbor. And though it was a shame, in Brooklyn, New York, in Compton, California, in Chicago, Illinois, in St. Louis, Missouri and every other ghetto neighborhood across America, someone always received that phone call. As Mrs. Fuller stared into the open space before her, she thought to herself, "It was supposed to be the other way around. I wasn't supposed to bury any of my children, my children were supposed to bury me."

CHAPTER NINETEEN

In the recovery section of the trauma unit at Kings County Hospital, a small number of family and friends of Barry Williams kept vigil at his bedside. After a successful operation, Daryl's close friend was listed in serious but stable condition.

Seventy-two hours had gone by and Daryl's lungs had collapsed three times. I was a mess. I hadn't been home since the shooting and I vowed not to leave Daryl's bedside until he was on the road to recovery. Fortunately, the children who attended the cookout were in the house playing video games during the time of the shootings so none of them witnessed the fracas. Daphne did hear the gunshots, but after she was safely escorted to my mother's home, word of the incident wasn't repeated and Daphne went about as if nothing ever happened.

The sudden knock at the door startled me and woke me up from my nap.

"Who is it?" I asked, hoping not to be bothered. My hair was a mess, and although I brushed my teeth and washed my face, I hadn't showered in the three days I'd been at the hospital and the sticky feeling I was experiencing wasn't soothing at all.

The knock came again and Barry wheeled himself into the room. "May I come in?" he pleasantly asked.

I grinned a faint smile as tears welled up in my eyes. I'd only been to see Barry once and that was when the doctors were operating on him. I stood up, walked over to Barry, leaned over and gave him a warm hug. I squeezed him tight, sniffed back tears, released him and asked him if he was okay.

"Yeah, I'm ahight. I'm good. I'm in a little pain, but the doctors said I should recover in no time. How about you? How are you holding up?" Barry's voice was sincere, warm. He was trying to be supportive, but being a victim himself, he could only do but so much.

I grinned that faint smile once again, shook my head without speaking and began to cry. Barry rolled closer to me. "I need him, Barry. Daphne needs him." I was holding him again and crying.

Daryl had tubes running all through him. He was connected to a respirator that was assisting him with his breathing and the oxygen cup that was placed over his nose and mouth seemed to swallow his entire face. The I.V. fed him to keep him strong, but the tiny drops of liquid didn't seem like enough. Daryl was used to solid foods, soul foods. The mere thought of my ex-husband, the only man I ever loved besides my father, whom I still loved dearly, having to live off liquids and artificial breathing apparatuses, made me sick to my stomach. I started to feel nauseous for the umpteenth time and asked Barry to excuse me. He did and I headed for the ladies room.

Barry stared at his friend and observed his poor health. He sighed and said, "Damn, homie." He sadly shook his head and prayed that his dear friend would pull through. While he sat helplessly in his wheelchair, Barry remembered the first time he and Daryl met. They both attended Martin Luther King, Jr. High School in downtown Manhattan. Daryl was a freshman and Barry was a junior. Both of them were from Brooklyn and both of them had the same gym class. Back then, Barry was a big bully. He saw Daryl as a potential target to prey upon since Daryl was new and only weighed about 120 pounds soaking wet. So one day, Barry approached him in the locker room. Daryl was digging in his locker when Barry crept up beside him, slammed the locker door shut, peered down on the new jack and said in a startling deep voice, "Nigga, my name is Big B and I'm from the Stuy! Do or die, nigga! Brooklyn! Where the fuck is you reppin'?" Barry had his peanut gallery with him who were on the side giggling.

To Barry's surprise, Daryl stood up on the bench, peered down at Barry and yelled back, "Nigga, my name is Daryl and I'm from Brooklyn too! The Ville, nigga! Never ran, never will! What!"

The two of them stood there for a moment staring at one another until Barry broke the ice with a smile. He held his hand out to Daryl and said, "Nice to meet you, homie. You lucky you ain't from Manhattan or you would've caught a beat down."

Daryl cracked a smile and returned the friendly gesture and on that day, the two of them became friends and as Barry would eventually say, "They became closer than ten fat people in an elevator."

But this wasn't the school locker room and they weren't still in King High School. Barry was in a wheelchair recovering from a gunshot wound and his best friend was possibly on his deathbed. It wasn't much Barry could do except talk to his unconscious homeboy. So he rolled as close to the bed as he possibly could, grabbed Daryl's hand and poured out his feelings. "Damn man. It seems like it was just yesterday when we first met." Barry smiled, but the pain in his stomach caused the smile to be quickly wiped away. "That time we went out to Miami seemed like it was just yesterday too. Damn, we had so much fun together. Especially with them Asian broads." Daryl made no attempt to respond. He didn't flinch or anything. But the machines kept his stomach pumping and his heart beating. Barry raised his hand to his face and dabbed the inner corners of his eyes, drying the tears that quickly built up over the last few minutes. "I never really told you this and I know you know, Daryl, but I love you, homie. Just like a brother," he sighed. "Come on, man, don't die on us. You got a beautiful daughter, an ex-wife who still loves you, and tons of friends who care about you. What's gonna happen to M & M if you ain't around to run it? Who's supposed to run it like you? Nobody. Nobody can run it like Big Dee." He sniffed back more tears. "I heard they killed that lil boy who shot us, but I think he was just scared. He was afraid of something and that boy made a bad decision, but I don't think he deserved to die like that. I heard those police shot that kid like he was a dog, man." Barry heard me reenter the room. "Listen, homie," he patted his pal's leg. "I'm here for you." He tapped his big broad chest where his heart was located and continued, "I'm right here, Dee." Barry slowly wheeled himself backwards then spun around. I hugged him again and watched him as he exited the room crying softly. I knew he was hurting because I felt the same way, if not worse.

I took my position beside my ex-husband, cupped his hand and looked at him. My tears flowed easily down my face since

I had no reason to hold back. I whispered, "Daryl. Daryl. Can you hear me?" I swallowed hard and raised my voice just a notch. "Daryl, I love you. I've never stopped loving you. I loved you from the first time I laid my eyes on you and I still loved you when we got our divorce. I loved you when I was pregnant, and I loved you when I was in labor for sixteen hours. I loved you under every circumstance, Daryl, and out of everything we've been through, this hurts the most, honey. I'm suffering right now. I can't sleep, I can't eat, I can't hold a simple cup of water, I can't even think straight." My cries increased. "Daryl, how are you going to leave me and Daphne? How are you gonna just leave us all alone? How are you gonna leave your queen? Your princess?" My voice became thin as if I were speaking in a high pitched whisper. "I can't live without you, Dee. I can't. I won't be able to function. These past three days have been killing me." I looked up towards the ceiling, then lowered my head to the bed railing and started wailing. "Whhyy? Whhyy are you making me suffer? Lord, why? What am I going to do without him? I swear to God, p...please! Please, God, I swear to you. I promise on everything." I was in a desperate state to the point that I was pleading with my Lord. "Please let him live. I'm begging you, Lord. I swear if you keep him with us, I won't ever leave his side." I banged my head on the bed railing over and over until I caused one of the monitors to beep, or so I thought.

"Beep...beep...beep...beep...beep...beep. Beepbeepbeep!"

"Oh, my God, oh, my God, I'm sorry. I'm sorry. God, please no, help! Help! Somebody help me!" I started screaming at the top of my lungs. I sounded like I was losing my mind. Truth is, I was.

Two nurses and a doctor ran into the room and asked me

what had happened. I explained and after the doctor checked Daryl's vitals, he turned to the nurses and said, "I don't believe it, he's stabilizing. His blood pressure is going down, his heart rate is evening out and his breathing is becoming more steady." Then he looked at me and said, "Ma'am, your husband is going to make it. He's going to be alright."

I couldn't believe it. I laughed, cried, then laughed again all in one breath. I thanked God over and over in my prayers and did my best to stick to my promise.

A year after Daryl was released from the hospital, he and I were remarried and living together again. We started all over and took things at a slower pace this time around.

"Dee, you know I willed your ass back to life, right?" I said smiling. We were cuddled up together on our living room sofa while Daphne took refuge on a blanket on the floor with a Sponge Bob toy in her hand.

"I know, baby girl. You brought Daddy's ass back from the dead."

"That's right." I ran my hands smoothly over his bald head. "I just refused to let you die because I knew I would've suffered miserably had I lost you."

He looked up at me. His head was in my lap. "So what you're saying is, you wouldn't have been able to live without me?"

"No, I would've lived, honey, but it wouldn't have been good for me or for Daphne. I wasn't willing to give up that easily. I wasn't. I refused to let that happen, plus I was tired of suffering. So I asked God to hook a sistah up and he looked out. Now it's me and you against the world." I smiled, bent down, placed my tongue in Daryl's mouth and clicked the light off. We continued to live happily ever after and I was never too far away from my husband.

THE END

FINAL WORD

To sum it all up, the key to any relationship is communication. Find out what makes your partner happy and what makes them sad. Find out what makes them whole and what makes them incomplete. What's not enough and what satisfies them. Keep an open mind and be mindful that someone else is in your equation. Don't give up so easily and always try and work things out. Life is the most beautiful thing God has created, love is the second and forgiveness, which is simply us accepting what happens, allows us to move on. We should practice them and cherish them our entire lives.

Acknowledgements

God first and foremost. Allah has blessed me in ways I never would have imagined. My mother, good looking out for being there every single time I needed you. Wifey, one day I sat wondering whether I was ever going to have the love I spread to so many others, reciprocated back to me. Then you sat down next to me and looked deep into my eyes. And there it was, the love given back to me in the form of your heart. My daughter, Amiaya, you're the princess in my kingdom. Thanks for giving our company a wonderful name, smile. My lil man, Jyamiene, you've always made Daddy proud of you. Keep up the good work. My sisters, Danita and Melsoultree. My brothers, Big Frank and Robert. My nieces, Tiarra, Tatiana, Danielle, Elexis and Big Frank's other daughters. My nephews, Lil Frank Nitty, Nerf, Jacques, Bochi and Big Frank's other sons. To my Co-Dee's, Dee, Buke, Slick, Jar,and Jus. To all of my mans on lock down. To all of my peoples in the Hood. To all of my readers, my fans, I love y'all. To all the bookstores that support me and all the vendors doing their thing. Shout to Tanya "Bx," our street team Queen. To my fellow authors that continue to show love, Moody Holiday ("Love's Twilight", "Wild Innocence, a Tale from the Eighties," and "Sweet Redemption"), Anthony Whyte ("Ghetto Girls"), Mark Anthony ("Dogism" and "Paper Chasers"), Angela Wallace ("Secret Dramas"), Vickie Stringer ("Triple Crown"), Shannon Holmes ("Triple Crown"), Zane ("The Heat Seekers"), Danielle Santiago ("little Ghetto Girl. A Harlem Story"), Treasure E. Blue ("Harlem Girl Lost"), Tracy Brown ("Black, Dime Piece"), "K'wan ("Gangsta", Road Dawgs"and "Street Dreams"), T.N. Baker ("Shiesty"), Ebony Stroman and Dante "T-Shoota" Clarke ("The Hood"), Erick S. Gray ("Booty Call"), Teri Woods ("True to the Game"), Jimmy DaSaint "Money, Desires, Regrets"), Tiffany Womble ("Liquid Dreams"),Crystal Lacey Winslow ("Life, Love and Loneliness, The Criss Cross), The Amiaya Entertainment Roster James 'I-GOD' Morris (A Diamond In The Rough, Broken Bonds-From The Wombs To The Tombs) Coming in 2005, G.B. Johnson (Against The Grain) 05', Ralph 'Polo' Taylor (All About The Paper)05', Travis 'Unqiue' Stevens (I'aint Mad At Ya)05', Teresa Aviles05', Thomas Glover (Sistah's)05', Vincent 'V.I.' Warren (Hoezetta)05', Angela Wallace05'.

To my Hood, as always, Edenwald: The Blue Park : Jesse, Jimmy, Fred (Prik), Nature, Michelob, Cahiem, Calil, Lil Richie,Big Richie Tee, George (Geo) McCoppin, Bert McCoppin, Beissy, Charlene, True, Ms. Holmes, Mario, Braindead & Jemel, Peaches, Paulette (Peaches), Moo Moo.

Trey Duece: Shakim, Beezo, Kevin Smith, Bert, Islam, Maine, Stephon and Mike Vernon, Pretty Black, Lamont, Bernard & Lil Mike, Bo-Pete (R.I.P.), P.J. (R.I.P), Kashiem , Plu, Drea and Ms. Flo, Gonzo, Chap, Ms. Lavern.

The Otano's: Jeanette, Margie, Francis, Stacey, Tonya, Liza, Jael, Mikey and my Goddaughter Shaun.

Nona and Niecey, Ronnie and Carol, K.K., Ice Cold, Moe, & Charlie, Tugah, Cynthia, Glenn & Michelle, Nay Nay and Lonzell, Fat Billy, Shameeka & Taniya, Ratboy, Byron, A.C., Fat Shawn, Mongo, Claire, P.O. & Vonell, Fat Hasan, Tuto, Tuto R.I.P, Belinda, Joe Joe R.I.P., The Horse Shoe, Bum Square, The Line, Lisa & Suyapa, Cynthia

1160: Butthead, Bummy, Kareem, Shawn Green, Ramel, Pop, Munchie, EEdee, Russell, **Kim Cabble,** Barry aka Noodles, Troy, Tony & Calito, Sonya, Ms. Regina, Marvin, Trent.

1170: Yah Yah, Fly Guy, Monique, Rev Gotti

1154: Treecie, Huggie, Shanequa, V.I., Sandra, Diedra, Mrs. Burke, Fat Danny, Michael Dawson, Michelle, Tanya Fergerson, Ann, Shannon (1st fl.), Reyna, Shaqeema, Cheryl & Collette, Quamay, Tee, Peanut, Marcus, Spofford.

1138: Diane, Samantha, Both Sets of Twins (Trina & Dina) and the Light Skinned Sisters, Tawanna, Craig, Dawn Doctor, Kevin Blackwood (R.I.P).

1141: The Ruler, The God Father, Big Ray, Geto, Randy, Big-B, Terrell, B.O., Box, Jimmy, Buck, Rob, Robot (R.I.P.), Dave & Chuck, Tara.

1135: Casper, Sugar Pop, Lil Ron, Ez, Tanya.

1175: The Naked Faces, Laura & Charlene, Cinnamin, Ronnie & Pete, Dornice & Sonny, Ticky

1173: Mary, Raquel and Freddy, Lil Raven and Justine, Sharissa, Champ Mc.

1159: Isidro (R.I.P), Teresa Aviles, Peanut, Big Jus, Fuquan (Dwayne Reed)

1137: Cassandra, Salihah, Kesha, Shanequa, Toya, John John, Kareem, Malik, Lamont

The Green Family: Downtown, Uptown, Imperial, Jemel,

Jamilah, Troy (R.I.P), Sabrina (R.I.P).

Jaime-O, Moe-Smash, Big Earl, Prince & Dre, Kesha, Don, Damon (R.I.P.), Dula, Angela, John Rambo, Prince Linton, Dog-Masood, True (Wear), DJ, Stink, Cash, Telisa Alston, My Cousins: Powerful, Shawn, Sharon, Cynthia, Rosalyn, Danielle, Ann, Aretha, Chris, Charlie, Danny, Dah Dah, April, Karen, Jennifer.

My man Shorts, Rock, Smoke, BZ, Malcolm (Black), Buffalo (Black), Poopie, Pam, Lodisha, Albanian Ock, Dardani, Jawad, Osirus (Shakur) Jackson, Jalil Jones, Junior Black, Eric Mobley, Darnell (Bike King), Shane Woney, Dylan Daniels, Yusef, Jr., Narvese, Louie & Isaiah, Evelyn, My nephew baby Jonathan, Nathan and Simon, Sean Brown, Bee, Diamond, Tange, Johnathan Gullery, Steve Apollo Pixel, Kenneth Carter, Leyda Diaz, Evelyn Diaz, Allison Godfrey, Kim Gay, Ely (Fordham Rd.), Blackstar (133rd & Lenox), Russell (149th Street third Ave., CD-125th Street, A&B Books, Culture Plus Books, Baker & Taylor,

Black Family Card (BX), Nubian Heritage (Harlem, Brooklyn and Queens), Hue-Man (125th Street), The IQ Spot (Manhattan), Da Streets Magazine, Black Horizon Books (Ryss), Major Books-Tri-State Mall (Delaware), African World Books (B-More), Walden's Book Stores, Amazon.com, The Black Library.com and Barnes and Noble.com. Big Shout out to Styles-P (The Lox) and Nicole Ray   (The R.O.C) for the Love.

Also, a special shout out to all the female prisoners all over the world. To all the women in Danbury, Alderson and Bedford Hills, ladies, I got crazy love for y'all. You women are incredible people. I have a tremendous amount of love and respect for you knowing how hard and stressful it can get at times. So to all my Black and Hispanic Queens in the system, Riker's Island, Up North, the Feds and to those of you at home enduring the struggle, keep y'all heads up. And know that when your peoples don't seem like they're thinking about you, ya boy Inch is. So holla at me, ya heard! Oh Yeah, Big Shout Out to Martha Stewart for taking that bid like a trooper.

One!

Fan Mail Page

If you have any further questions, comments or concerns, kindly address your inquires in care of:

Antoine "Inch" Thomas

At

AMIAYA ENTERTAINMENT LLC
P.O.BOX 1275
NEW YORK, NY 10159

tanianunez79@hotmail.com

Flower's Bed

The Most Controversial Book Of This Era

Written By

Antoine "Inch" Thomas

Suspenseful...Fastpaced...Richly Textured

PUBLISHED BY AMIAYA ENTERTAINMENT

From the Underground Bestseller "Flower's Bed"
Author Antoine "Inch" Thomas delivers you

NO REGRETS

It's Time To Get It Popping

"Gritty....Realistic Conflicts....Intensely Eerie"
Published by Amiaya Entertainment

COMING SOON

FROM AMIAYA ENTERTAINMENT LLC

THAT
GANGSTA SH!T!

The Anthology

Featuring Stories
by
Antoine Inch Thomas

www.amiayaentertainment.com

ORDER FORM

Number of Copies

Unwilling To Suffer	ISBN# 0-9745075-2-0	$15.00/Copy _____
No Regrets	ISBN# 0-9745075-1-2	$14.95/Copy _____
Flower's Bed	ISBN# 0-9745075-0-4	$14.95/Copy _____

Mailing Options

PRIORITY POSTAGE (4-6 DAYS US MAIL): Add $4.95

Accepted form of Payments: Institutional Checks or Money Orders

(All Postal rates are subject to change.)

Please check with your local Post Office for change of rate and schedules.

Please Provide Us With Your Mailing Information:

SHIPPING ADDRESS

Name:_____

Address:_____

Suite/Apartment#:_____

City:_____

Zip Code:_____

(Federal & State Prisoners, Please include your Inmate Registration #)

SEND CHECKS OR MONEY ORDERS TO:

AMIAYA ENTERTAINMENT

P.O.BOX 1275

NEW YORK, NY 10159

212-946-6565

www.amiayaentertainment.com

MelSoulTree

Some say she's an R& B Soul singer with a Gospel twist. Others say she is an R&B Soul Singer with a Jazzy twist. Yet, everyone agrees she is **MelSoulTree...Melissa ROOTED in SOUL!!!** **MelSoulTree's** melodious voice and vocal range has been compared to the likes of Minnie Riperton, Phyllis Hyman, Chaka Kahn, Alicia Keys and Mariah Carey. In order to capture the true essence of her voice you have to experience her "live" or listen to one of her recordings.

This talented vivacious beauty hails from NYC's borough of the Bronx. Born Melissa Antoinette Thomas she began to develop her love for music at the tender age of 4. She was exposed to different styles of music via the radio, her father (a poet & musician), her mother (a singer) and a musical family rooted in R&B Soul, Gospel, Jazz and Hip Hop music styles. **MelSoulTree** has been blanketed with music all her life. Despite all her influences she began studying to become an attorney. However, the call of music was so strong it dismissed that idea right away! By pursuing her love of music, her singing talents have taken her to places that one could only dream of. She has established herself as a gifted singer and songwriter. As an international artist she has toured extensively throughout Germany, France, Switzerland, Argentina, Uruguay, Chile, Canada and many areas of the U.S. as a featured soloist singing R&B, Jazz and Gospel music.

Some of **MelSoulTree's** many accomplishments include:
Graduating at the top of her Music class in the area of Jazz Vocal Music from the City College of New York under the direction of vocalist **Sheila Jordan** and bassist **Ron Carter.**
Working with the legendary **D.J. Grand Master Flash** and being featured on the chart topping **"New Jack City"** movie soundtrack song **"Lyrics 2 the Rhythm"** produced by the **Giant/Warner** label.
Recording for the **Wild Pitch**, **Audio Quest** and **Select** Record labels.
Honored to work with **William "Smokey" Robinson** and **William "Mickey" Stevenson** in their Musical Stage play **"Raisin' Hell".**
Former lead vocalist for the underground New York City based band **Special Request.**
Former lead singer and songwriter for the **Lo-Key Records** female group **Legal Tender.**
One of the youngest members to sing with the **Duke Ellington Orchestra** under the direction of **Paul Ellington.**
A frequent featured soloist for the **Princeton Jazz Orchestra.**
Although born long after the 60's era, she is currently one of the youngest singers touring with the world renowned Phil Spector's group **"The Crystals"**. She is known affectionately as "The Kid" by many of the veterans of the music business.

Can you believe most of these accomplishments where achieved as an unsigned artist? She is now establishing herself as one of the most sought after independent solo artists. Experience her for yourself during one of her live performances or again and again on CD. Don't miss the opportunity of witnessing the unique sound and vocal range of **MelSoulTree... Melissa ROOTED in SOUL!!!**

For CD, ticket and booking information use one of the following contact methods:

On the WEB...*visit one of the secure* <u>*MelSoulTree Websites:*</u>
www.soundclick.com/MelSoulTree
www.MelSoulTree.com

**FOR MAIL ORDER FORMS &
FAN CLUB INFORMATION...**

MelSoulTree
P.O. Box 46
New York, NY 10475

**The MelSoulTree/Granted Entertainment Hotline...
(212) 560-7117**
Coming in 2005...the long awaited album introducing...
MelSoulTree...Melissa ROOTED in SOUL!!!